BLO

"Look at the bloo[...]d. "They're practically empty. Here. Look at the inferior vena cava."

He indicated a flattened gray tube running down the back of the abdominal wall. "Normally it's full of blood," he said.

Jean felt the hairs on the back of her neck standing up, as if she were in the presence of something frightening, something evil and silent emanating from the open body.

"Let's see . . ." Dr. Anderson picked up the chart, flipped through the pages until he came to the anesthesia record. "The anesthetist estimated blood loss at about 750 mls, which is about a pint and a half. . . ." Dr. Anderson stared at the chart, then at Jean.

"There's hardly any blood in this body," he said. "I don't understand this at all. Apparently he didn't bleed that much during the operation. . . . He wasn't shot or stabbed. . . ."

Jean noticed his nervous grin—it was obvious that he was seriously shaken. "This is very strange," he said. "Bloody strange."

A TANGLED KNOT OF MURDER

A Dr. Jean Montrose Mystery

by
C. F. Roe

A SIGNET BOOK

SIGNET
Published by the Penguin Group
Penguin Books USA Inc., 375 Hudson Street,
New York, New York 10014, U.S.A.
Penguin Books Ltd, 27 Wrights Lane,
London W8 5TZ, England
Penguin Books Australia Ltd, Ringwood,
Victoria, Australia
Penguin Books Canada Ltd, 10 Alcorn Avenue,
Toronto, Ontario, Canada M4V 3B2
Penguin Books (N.Z.) Ltd, 182–190 Wairau Road,
Auckland 10, New Zealand

Penguin Books Ltd, Registered Offices:
Harmondsworth, Middlesex, England

First published by Signet, an imprint of Dutton Signet,
a division of Penguin Books USA Inc.

First Printing, December, 1996
10 9 8 7 6 5 4 3 2 1

 REGISTERED TRADEMARK—MARCA REGISTRADA

Printed in the United States of America

PUBLISHER'S NOTE
This is a work of fiction. Names, characters, places, and incidents either are the product of the author's imagination or are used fictitiously, and any resemblance to actual persons, living or dead, events, or locales is entirely coincidental.

BOOKS ARE AVAILABLE AT QUANTITY DISCOUNTS WHEN USED TO PROMOTE PRODUCTS OR SERVICES. FOR INFORMATION PLEASE WRITE TO PREMIUM MARKETING DIVISION, PENGUIN BOOKS USA INC., 375 HUDSON STREET, NEW YORK, NEW YORK 10014.

A TANGLED
KNOT
OF MURDER

Chapter 1

"You have a new patient, Dr. Montrose."

It wasn't so much the words as Eleanor's inflection that made Dr. Jean Montrose look up. Eleanor, her longtime secretary, who also did the job of nurse when needed, poked her head through the doorway into Jean's office.

"So?" Jean asked, smiling. "You make it sound as if it's the first time we had a new patient in fifteen years."

"First time we've had one like this," said Eleanor darkly. She glanced behind her at the closed waiting room door. "It's Robertson Kelso."

That got Jean's attention. "Him? Not Irene or Jeff?"

"Himself. He's got a bellyache and says he's dying. Best thing that could happen to him, is what I think ..."

"Now, Eleanor ..." said Jean in a tut-tutting tone, and she glanced at the door, as if Robertson Kelso might suddenly appear and come barging in to her office. Even with a bellyache bad enough to make him see a doctor, Robertson Kelso was still a frightening man. If he said he was dying, and if that wasn't just one of Eleanor's exaggerations, he probably had something seriously the matter with him.

"You'd better put him in the exam room," she told Eleanor. "I'll see him as soon as I've finished this report."

Five minutes later, Jean stood up, sighed, and her mind turned to her new patient: Robertson Kelso. If she hadn't felt so sorry for his wife and their son, Jeff, she would probably have told him to go find himself another doctor. She had never actually done that, not in all her years in practice, but Robertson Kelso was very different, and she shied away from the thought of having to talk to him, let alone physically touch him.

She took her white coat off the hook on the back of the door and pulled it on. She didn't use it much these days, but now the white cotton coat felt like a kind of protection, something that would distance her from Robertson Kelso, like holding a cross when approaching a vampire. Eleanor, waiting at her desk, followed Jean into the examining room.

The man was lying on the exam table, partially covered by a sheet. He was a big, burly, red-faced fellow in his mid-thirties, with a pockmarked complexion that told of severe, healed adolescent acne, and thick, muscular arms. Now he was grunting with the pain in his belly, and had pulled his legs up to ease it. It had started a few hours ago, he told Jean. An intermittent cramping pain at first, it had grown worse and for the last hour hadn't let up at all.

"Did Irene or Jeff have anything like this? Or vomiting, or diarrhea?" she asked, thinking it might be a salmonella infection from something they had all eaten. She tried to stay objective and polite with him, but it was an effort to keep the coldness out of her voice.

"No. They're all right."

Jean examined him, feeling unhappy about having to touch his body, but it didn't take her long to reach a conclusion. "I think you have appendicitis," she said, stepping back. "You need to go up to the hospital."

Kelso muttered something. He obviously wasn't happy with the diagnosis.

Jean ignored what she half heard. "Is there somebody who can take you up there?"

"I have a car outside. One of my people drove me here."

"Good. I'll call the hospital and tell them to expect you."

Eleanor went out to tell the driver to come and help get Kelso to the car.

While Jean waited for the hospital operator to answer, she asked, "And how's Irene?"

"She's fine."

"Still bumping into things?" Jean's voice was sharp and contemptuous.

Kelso grinned through his pain, an ugly grin that showed a lot of small teeth.

"Yes," he said, "she's still as stupid, and she's still bumping into things."

"And Jeff?" He's still bumping into things, too?"

"Yes. All the time. Amazing, isn't it?" He gave Jean a penetratingly aggressive, mean stare.

My God, she thought, how could that poor timid Irene Kelso keep on living with this monster?

Mr. Hugh Kirkwall was not happy about being summoned to the hospital, although he was on call, and after all those years he should have been used to it. He left the Isle of Skye Lounge and got into his car, slamming the door closed. Damn it, he thought, reaching for the roll of mints in the glove compartment, sometimes I really detest this job. You didn't use to detest it, said a quiet voice inside his head as he nosed the car out of the hotel parking area into the Dundee Road. In fact, you loved it, until ... At that moment a huge white tour bus flew past in front of him, missing his car by inches. The wind of its passing rocked his car, and Hugh was shaken. He hadn't seen the bus until it was almost on top of him, and he should have, although the lights reflecting off the puddles at the side of the road had dazzled him. And he shouldn't have drunk more than a couple of Macallans when he knew he was on call ... Of course this wasn't exactly the first time he'd been caught out like this, but fortunately there had never been any trouble. Well, that wasn't exactly true, either.

There *had* been trouble, not even that long ago. It hadn't been terrible, nobody had died or anything, but the incident had attracted enough attention that he'd received a reluctant but stern warning from Sandy Michie, the hospital administrator. Crossing the old Tay bridge into Perth, Hugh thought for a moment of going home and phoning his colleague Frank Grant to ask him to take the call, then he remembered that Frank was away on vacation. The only other person who could have helped out was old Dr. Lumsden, but he was on the verge of retiring, and anyway he was sick with the flu. And that was why he, Hugh, was on call for the second night running.

He had been sitting by himself at the bar, drinking quietly, when the pay phone near the door had rung. Samson, the barman, had hesitated, waiting to see if Hugh would answer it, but Hugh went on doing what he'd been doing for the last hour, staring into his drink. So Samson wiped his hands on a towel and came around the bar to pick up the phone.

"It's for you, Hugh," he said quietly. "It's the hospital."

For a moment Hugh was tempted to shake his head, indicate to Samson that he wasn't here. Then his conscience and his training kicked in, and he slowly stood up and took the phone, which Samson was silently holding out to him.

"Can't it keep until the morning?" he'd asked Dr. Shah, the emergency room doctor who had summoned him. Dr. Shah—Dr. Ramashandra

Shah—had not been as circumlocutory as usual. "If you don't come in, Mr. Kirkwall," he had said in that high, piping Bombay English, "I will be forced to report your refusal to Mr. Michie." And after that conversation, it was too late to complain of a stomach upset or anything like that. There was nothing else for it—he just had to drive to the hospital, see the patient and as few other people as possible, prescribe something for him, then get out of there and go home.

Hugh put another peppermint in his mouth.

He tried to remember how long Shah had been working in the emergency room at the Perth Royal Infirmary. It must have been about three years, he thought, turning left at the roundabout. Over to his right Hugh could see the lights of the six-storied police headquarters, and he reminded himself to drive carefully; he'd been stopped a couple of weeks before, and only the fact that he'd once operated on the policeman's father had saved him from being arrested. He wouldn't have that kind of luck twice. His mind turned back to the arrogant Dr. Shah, and unconsciously Hugh's fist balled up. At first, Shah had only worked part-time at Perth Royal Infirmary, because he was OB/GYN trained and worked two days a week at a Dundee clinic. However, about a year ago, he'd given up his Dundee job and was now employed full-time at PRI. But Shah's main preoccupation in life seemed to be to harass Hugh as much as possible.

Hugh made it up the hill to the hospital without

incident, but as he made the sharp left turn into the hospital grounds, the back wheels of the car mounted the high pavement around the gates and the vehicle lurched, almost out of control. Hugh thought he was going to hit the ambulance outside the emergency entrance, but he managed to steer around it, drove past the entrance, and came to a safe stop in the doctors' parking area. He switched off the engine and sat there for a few moments, sweating. That would have been the last straw, he thought, if he'd hit the ambulance. He'd already lost some loyal friends in the last year, and now there were people in the hospital hierarchy who would use any such incident to try to get him thrown off the staff. Well, he thought grimly, they'd been trying to do that for a while, but so far, they hadn't succeeded, and he was still there.

Hugh stumbled a bit coming out of his car, but he pulled himself together, kept his gaze fixed on the well-lit double doors, and walked with a deliberate step, very straight toward the hospital entrance.

Dr. Shah smiled when he saw Hugh come through the doors; it wasn't a friendly smile, but prim, humorless, and calculating, and his eyes were cold and observant behind his thick glasses.

"Yes, Mr. Kirkwall, thank you for coming." To Hugh's hypersensitive ear, the way he said "Mr." made it sound like an insult, although it was the traditional appellation of surgeons in Britain, and one they were very proud of. Shah glanced at the clock as if he were making a note of the time,

which in fact he was. He had first called Mr. Kirkwall forty-eight minutes earlier. Shah stood up behind the desk, putting his hands together with
fraudulent humility. "This is the case of a thirty-
four-year-old male whose chief complaint is abdominal pain. This pain started this afternoon and
was originally crampy in character . . ."

"Doesn't this thirty-four-year-old male have a
name?" asked Hugh, making no effort to hide his
contempt for Shah's impersonal attitude to his patients. "I know that to you people they're just
numbers, but our quaint local custom here is to
give people names." Hugh glowered, red-eyed, at
Dr. Shah.

Dr. Shah glanced at the chart with a poorly dis-
guised smirk, as if he'd been waiting for this moment. "Yes, sir, his name is Robertson Kelso, sir.
His pain . . ."

Hugh started. "Robertson Kelso? Jesus Christ,
that . . ."

"Yes, sir." Shah stared contentedly at Hugh,
happy that part of his mission had been accom-
plished. "As I was saying, Mr. Kelso's pain was
originally crampy in character . . ." Dr. Shah went
on in his singsong voice, slightly but noticeably
accenting Kelso's name. "Then, about three hours
ago, the pain became more severe, located in his
right lower quadrant. He has a slight fever, of one
hundred degrees Fahrenheit. Physical examination
reveals severe tenderness in the right lower quadrant, with some rigidity . . ."

"What did you find on rectal examination?" asked Hugh.

"That procedure was deferred until your arrival, Mr. Kirkwall," said Dr. Shah smoothly.

Hugh grunted something. His hesitation and obvious discomfort made Shah smile covertly to himself.

"Well, I'd better go and see him, then," said Hugh.

"He's in the second booth on the right."

Hugh was already walking away from him. Dr. Shah watched him, observing the not-quite-steady way he walked. He'd already noticed that the surgeon's breath smelled of whiskey, and that too would be in his report.

Hugh pulled the green curtain. The man was lying on a stretcher, his breath fast and shallow. His eyes dilated slightly when he saw Hugh.

"Well, Kelso," said Hugh after staring at the man for a long moment, "you must be about as happy to see me as I am to see you."

"Just take care of my problem." Kelso tried to move, and grunted with pain.

Hugh pulled the sheet off him and looked at his belly, covered with curly black hair. Like an ape, Hugh thought, hating the man.

"Have you ever had any pain like this before?"

Kelso shook his head. "Never. It's the worst pain I've ever had."

"Eaten anything that could have upset you?"

Again, Kelso shook his head.

"I'm going to examine you."

Hugh pulled a stethoscope out of his pocket and listened perfunctorily to Kelso's chest. Then he listened a bit more carefully to his belly, and heard nothing, no gurgles or rumbles. That was a bad sign, and he pursed his lips. Hugh had a lot of experience, and already he'd seen enough to know that Kelso was really sick. He tried not to feel any satisfaction from it.

He put a hand on Kelso's belly. It was as hard as iron, and not simply because he was a muscular man. When Hugh pulled his probing fingers away suddenly from the right side, Kelso groaned with the sudden exacerbation of pain.

Five minutes later, after a rectal exam which confirmed that Kelso had severe tenderness on the right side, Hugh stood up straight. "You've got appendicitis," he said. "We'll have to take you upstairs and get it out before it bursts."

"Do whatever you need to do," replied Kelso through clenched teeth. "I can't take much more of this."

"Did your wife come in with you?" Hugh kept the contempt and anger from showing in his voice. Kelso was now a patient, and whatever personal problems he had with him would be in abeyance until he was discharged.

"She's on her way," he said.

"Who's your family doctor?"

"Dr. Montrose," he replied. "I went to see her this afternoon, and she told me to come up here."

Hugh went back to the desk and told Doris Caie, the staff nurse, to call the evening supervisor and get the preparations for surgery under way. The theatre crew and the anaesthetist had to be called in, he reminded her. "As soon as possible," he said, then scribbled a brief note in Kelso's chart. That done, he went up to the doctors' lounge, which was as usual deserted at this time, turned the overhead lights off, sat down in one of the easy chairs, and went to sleep.

Back in the emergency room, Doris Caie checked the chart to see if Mr. Kirkwall had got the patient to sign the operation permission form. He hadn't, and with a sigh she went along the corridor, did her best to explain to Mr. Kelso what the operation consisted of, and got him to sign the form. He was having so much pain by then that she felt he would have signed anything. She put her initials next to his scrawled signature, and inserted the completed form in the chart. She knew that strictly speaking it wasn't her job to do that, but it had to be done, and they all knew that Mr. Kirkwall wasn't always entirely reliable, especially after a few Macallans. A little later, when Doris needed some help, she checked the typed list on the notice board and was glad to see that Rosemary Gallacher was on as evening supervisor.

Rosemary usually came down to the emergency room a couple of times during her shift, because things had a habit of changing quickly down there, and occasionally she had to move someone, a nurse or an aide, from elsewhere in the hospital when things got too busy. She really preferred to help out herself. Rosemary had worked for years in Emergency before becoming a supervisor, and they knew and liked her there. When things got hot in Emergency, Rosemary would just roll up her sleeves and pitch in until the problem was dealt with. Afterward, when things calmed down and there was time for a cup of tea and a wee chat, Rosemary always made a point of spending a few minutes talking with the staff and hearing about their problems before going back on her rounds.

So Doris was relieved when Rosemary answered the summons, and came marching down the corridor from the main part of the hospital toward the emergency desk. Rosemary was a big, solid, square-faced woman in her early forties, and one of the few who still wore the traditional nursing cap over her graying hair, which she made no effort to hide or color. Rosemary's natural expression was kindly but reserved; as befitted her position, she was a serious, intense, and capable person.

"Mrs. Gallacher, we have this patient going up to surgery," said Doris rather hesitantly. "He's having a lot of pain, and I wondered if we could give him some Demerol or something."

"Have you asked his doctor?"

"Well, it's Mr. Kirkwall, and I can't find him." Doris looked embarrassed. "He's here in the hospital somewhere, and I'm sure you heard me page him. Maybe he's upstairs in the doctors' lounge."

Rosemary frowned. "How about Dr. Shah?" she

asked. "Couldn't he have prescribed something for the patient?"

Doris shifted her feet. "Well, I asked him, but Dr. Shah says that he's handed the case over to Mr. Kirkwall, and from now on any medicines should be prescribed by him."

Rosemary sighed, knowing of the hostility between the two physicians, and thought about the good old days when the patient's welfare was put before any petty squabbles among the staff. "Okay ... Let me see the chart."

Doris passed it over quickly, as if she were transferring the entire responsibility for the patient to her supervisor.

Rosemary opened the chart, and drew in her breath suddenly when she saw the patient's name. Doris watched her face expectantly, but Rosemary just went through the papers, then put the chart down and said, "I'll go and find Mr. Kirkwall. Meanwhile, Doris, please give the patient 100 milligrams of Demerol intramuscularly, and I'll make sure Mr. Kirkwall signs for it."

Relieved, Doris went off to get the medication, and Rosemary checked the schedule to see who was on call for anesthesia. She was relieved to see that it was Anna McKenzie, a very capable young woman with plenty of experience, and who, Rosemary suspected, felt strongly about Hugh Kirkwall, in spite of his recent troubles. And the scrub nurse on call was Beulah Falconer; and that was a blessing, too, because she was very competent and knew how to keep Mr. Kirkwall out of trouble. Just then the outside door opened and the two of them came in, Anna McKenzie and Beulah Falconer. Rosemary told them what the situation was, then picked up the chart and marched down the corridor to find Mr. Kirkwall, a look of tight-lipped determination on her face.

Doris Caie, now alone behind the long desk, looked quickly around. Dr. Shah was back in the doctors' room and the door was closed. To her left, Beulah Falconer, Anna McKenzie, and Rosemary Gallacher were disappearing down the long corridor. Doris picked up the telephone, dialed 9 for an outside line, then called a local number.

"Hello?" she said in a quiet voice, and when she heard the other person answer, she looked around again, then said, "Albert, you'll never guess who came into the hospital tonight. Robertson Kelso."

Chapter 2

When Rosemary found Hugh Kirkwall, he was still in the doctors' lounge. She put the light on. He sat up in the easy chair, blinked, stared at her for a moment, evidently not quite sure where he was. "Oh," he mumbled, "I think I was asleep." His voice was a little slurred, and Rosemary had to work hard to hide her annoyance with him. Hugh had fallen a long way. A good surgeon, he had been a power in the hospital and popular with everyone—until he started drinking. And now here he was, the surgeon on call, with people's lives in his hands, having drunk alcohol to the point where he probably wasn't safe to drive a car, let alone operate on anyone. Rosemary felt very frustrated, and under other circumstances she would have politely told him that in her opinion, he should just go home; then she would have called in whoever was next on the surgical roster. But tonight, of all nights, there wasn't anybody else.

"Your patient will be ready shortly, Mr. Kirkwall," she said in her stolid, matter-of-fact way.

She looked squarely at him. "There's some black coffee up in the changing room; it might help you to wake up."

"I'm awake, and I don't need any help," replied Hugh, sensing the reproof in her voice. "Is the theatre crew here yet?"

"They got here a few minutes ago," said Rosemary. "Anna McKenzie and Beulah Falconer. We're sending the patient upstairs now. By the way, you ordered some Demerol for him but didn't sign the order form. Here it is." She went over and held out the chart.

"I need my glasses," said Hugh, looking at the chart.

"They're in your pocket, Mr. Kirkwall."

"Oh, yes, of course . . ." Hugh pulled the glasses out of his breast pocket, adjusted them, and scribbled his initials under the order, without even reading it. "Thanks, Rosemary. Well, I'd better get myself upstairs." He heaved himself to his feet and stumbled. "I'm all right," he said gruffly, seeing her expression. "I only had a couple of drinks," he said, trying to sound as if he'd been drinking diluted orange juice, "and it's pretty well worn off by now."

"I hope so," replied Rosemary, her eyes cold. She turned at the door. "Did you remember to phone Mr. Kelso's doctor? Dr. Montrose?"

Hugh didn't answer, but picked up the phone, dialed 9 for an outside line, then hesitated.

"It's four three four six three," said Rosemary,

who knew the phone numbers of most of the doctors in town.

Mr. Kirkwall dialed it. "Jean? Yes, this is Hugh Kirkwall. I've seen your patient Robertson Kelso, and I think he has acute appendicitis. Yes. We're going to go ahead and take it out tonight. Actually, we'll be starting in a few minutes ..." He glanced at Rosemary, who nodded, then he went on, "I'll give you a call if we find anything unusual, okay?"

He hung up, and without looking at Rosemary, went off to the changing room, his back slightly hunched, a premonition of disaster heavy upon him.

By the time Hugh got to the operating theatre, Robertson Kelso was already on the table, and Anna McKenzie was talking quietly to him, gently placing a mask over his face. "It's just oxygen, Mr. Kelso," she said in her trained, soothing voice. "Take a deep breath, now, as deep as you can."

In the scrub room, Hugh soaped and scrubbed his hands while he watched through the big window at the controlled activity inside the theatre. This wouldn't do, and he knew it. He had to stop drinking. He knew how much resentment and concern it caused in the hospital, particularly among the staff who had to work with him. Even the ones who used to be his good friends didn't stop to chat in the corridors anymore. Sandy Michie, the hospital administrator, had warned him that if there were any more problems of that kind, action would have to be taken.

And of course there was Dr. Shah, waiting and scheming. Again, Hugh's soapy hands turned into fists when he thought about him. Shah, that bastard. Ever since he came to Perth from Bombay or wherever it was that he'd been spawned, Shah had tried to undermine him. Shah did everything by the book, knew every hospital regulation and bylaw by heart, and was intolerant of everything that hadn't been officially approved or anyone who didn't do everything by the book. He didn't like Hugh's methods, his approach, and resented his popularity with the patients. But he did like the fact that Hugh had started to drink too much, because he could use it as a weapon against him.

Shah was ambitious, always trying to get himself appointed to the major hospital committees, and had developed a reputation as a relentless seeker after power. Hugh, who had long been either a member or chairman of the more important hospital committees, was in serious danger of losing his place and his influence to Shah, partly because of his drinking, and in part because of Shah's persistence, his knowledge of the rules and regulations, and his stubborn unwillingness to compromise. Hugh shut off the water with his knee and backed through the door into the theatre, his hands elevated. Once Shah came after you, he thought, drying his hands on the sterile towel proffered by Beulah Falconer, you were in trouble.

Of course, Hugh wasn't exactly defenseless, either. He was a local boy, and that counted for a lot in Perth, and particularly at the Royal Infirmary. Also he was a native Scot, white, a member of the Church of Scotland, and he'd done most of his surgical training in Scotland, at the Western Infirmary in Glasgow. Perth was his place, his town, whereas Shah was just a visitor, not particularly trusted by the local citizenry, and certainly not liked, because of the arrogant, patronizing way he dealt with them.

Beulah had already draped the patient, and when Hugh, fully gowned, stepped up to the table, she stood opposite him, assuming the dual roles of assistant and scrub nurse. She'd helped him through cases before, and now she was unobtrusively evaluating his condition by the way he spoke and the way he picked up the instruments. She decided that on this occasion he would get by. His breath smelled of mints, but as a rule, even when he was visibly intoxicated, he didn't smell of liquor. Beulah had heard somewhere that single malt whiskies didn't come out on the breath as much as the blends. It was such a pity about him, she thought. He's a good surgeon and a nice man when he's sober; but now it was getting to be a major problem, and sooner or later someone would blow the whistle, or something awful would happen while he was operating. Beulah just hoped it wasn't going to be tonight.

"Everything all right at your end?" Hugh asked Anna on the other side of the ether screen.

"Fine." Anna came from the Western Isles, and had the soft, lilting voice native to those regions.

"He's asleep, if you want to go ahead." She smiled at him. Ever since coming to Perth, Anna had had a crush on Hugh, and was saddened and alarmed by what was happening to him.

"Knife." Hugh took a deep breath, determined to ignore the fact that it was Robertson Kelso he was operating on, and made a quick three-inch incision in the abdomen, below and to the right of the umbilicus.

"Clamps."

Beulah was already busy clamping the small bleeding vessels, but she stopped to pass him a clamp, indicating that from now on he could take them off the tray himself. He grinned at her over his mask. They had often worked together, and knew each other pretty well. He cut the thin outer layers of muscle, then separated the deeper fleshy ones with his fingers until he could see the white membranous peritoneum. Once he was through that, he would be inside the abdominal cavity, and what he found there would decide how things were going to go with this patient. If there was pus inside the cavity, that would mean that the appendix had ruptured, and that would convert it into a much more serious case.

"I need you to retract, hard," he told Beulah, who picked up two right-angled retractors and positioned one on each side of the incision. It was difficult, because the patient had such big and powerful muscles.

"Could you relax him a bit?" he asked Anna.

Anna nodded. "Sure. I'll give him twenty milligrams of succinylcholine," she said, and injected the potent, fast-acting muscle relaxant into Kelso's veins. "It'll take about a minute," she said. Anna was a typical Western Isler, thought Hugh. Quiet, competent, and doesn't say anything that doesn't need to be said. He had no idea that she felt so strongly about him.

When the muscles were sufficiently relaxed, Hugh picked up the peritoneal membrane with a pair of forceps and tented it up, away from the intestines. With the other hand he made a small opening with sharp-pointed scissors.

So far, so good, thought Beulah. He's doing okay. But there was a tension in the room, always present nowadays when Hugh Kirkwall was operating. There was some fluid inside the belly cavity, but no pus. Beulah put the right-angled retractors inside the abdomen, and Hugh put a couple of fingers in the opening, feeling among the slithery intestines for the inflamed appendix.

"Thought I had it there," he said after a minute or two.

Moments passed, and Hugh seemed to be getting anxious.

Beulah did her best to increase the size of the opening by pulling on the retractors, but to no avail. A line of sweat appeared on Hugh's forehead, wetting the edge of the paper cap.

"Hold the retractors for a minute," said Beulah.

Hugh took them, and Beulah put her smaller hand into the incision. She was tactful enough not to find the appendix immediately.

"Here, is this it?" she asked him.

Hugh peered at the incision. "I think so," he said. "Pass me a Babcock's." Beulah, who couldn't let go of the appendix at this moment, nodded to where the Babcock clamps were, and he picked it up himself, then using the curved tip of the clamp, grasped the inflamed appendix, now swollen to the size of the cap on a fountain pen.

"Got it?" asked Beulah.

"Got it," he said with satisfaction. "It's hot, all right. Here, look. See that green part near the tip? Another couple of hours, it would have burst."

Beulah, who knew that as well as he did, made awed noises, mostly to reassure everyone else in the room.

"Okay, Falconer," he said, trying to be light-hearted, "let's have a little less of your cheek, please." Hugh clamped the small artery to the appendix, cut it, and quickly tied it off with a black silk thread. Then he placed two heavy clamps across the base of the appendix and cut between them, removing the offending organ. Then he tied off the base of the appendix with a thick catgut tie, and took off the clamp.

"Now," he said to Beulah, "I'll hold the stump up while you put in the purse-string suture around it."

Beulah took the needle holder, in whose jaws were clamped a curved needle with a black silk thread, and carefully put in a circular purse-string stitch all around the base of the appendix.

"Tie it."

Beulah tied the suture while Hugh cut the threads to the stump of the appendix, which he then inverted, so that the stump was snugly enclosed within the purse-string suture.

"We'll be another five minutes," he said over the ether screen to Anna.

She nodded, and started to lighten the anesthetic. Hugh was usually pretty accurate, and she made it a point of pride to have the patient wake up just after the last skin clip had been placed.

About two minutes later, Anna looked over the screen and pulled the earpieces of her stethoscope out of her ears. "We have a problem, Hugh," she said. "His blood pressure's going down." She turned to the circulating nurse. "Hang up another liter of Ringer's lactate, please."

"What is it now?"

"His pressure? Ninety over forty. It was a hundred and twenty over eighty until a couple of minutes ago."

Hugh was sweating again, and his hand, the one grasping the needle holder, shook. "What's his ECG like?"

"Normal. I think he's probably bleeding."

"Oh, shit," muttered Hugh, his voice barely audible. He looked at Beulah.

"We'll have to reopen him," she said, ostensibly speaking to Anna. She knew there wasn't time to discuss it, and handed Hugh a pair of heavy scissors to cut the stitches that had already been placed.

He hesitated, and she took the scissors out of

his hands and cut the stitches holding the muscle layers together, and pulled the incision open again. As soon as the peritoneal stitches were cut, blood welled up from inside the belly.

"Suction," said Hugh, taking over again, sort of. But finally Beulah had to put her hand in and extract the cecum, to which the appendix had been attached. They found the stump of the artery to the appendix; somehow the tie had come off and it was pumping away into the belly. Once they found the problem, it was easy enough to take care of it. Hugh put in a double stitch around the stump of the artery so that it wouldn't reopen, and once again they closed the abdomen.

"How much blood do you think he lost?" asked Anna.

"Hard to tell," mumbled Hugh, who was putting in the skin clips. "Maybe a pint."

Anna looked at Beulah, who discreetly held up two fingers, indicating that two pints was probably closer to the mark.

"You want to give him blood?" asked Anna.

"No," said Hugh. "He's young, and he's healthy. He'll make it up in a week or two."

Beulah looked at Anna and shrugged slightly. They both knew that one of the reasons Hugh didn't want to give Kelso a blood transfusion was because it would show up on the hospital statistics, and he would need to explain why a transfusion had been necessary during a simple appendectomy.

"Okay," said Anna. "You're the boss."

As they put in the last clip and Beulah was putting on the dressing, Hugh got another nasty shock. He turned around to see the grim-faced Dr. Shah, clad in surgical greens, standing behind him. Rosemary Gallacher, who had changed also into operating garb, was there, too; they had apparently come unnoticed into the operating theatre, and judging from their expressions, they had both witnessed the entire frightening fiasco.

Chapter 3

"What do you want?" Hugh asked Dr. Shah, his voice high with tension. "You don't belong here, and you've got no right to come wandering into the theatre without my permission."

Dr. Shah stared at Hugh but didn't answer. After a few moments he turned and walked out.

Rosemary, always there when she was needed, helped the nurses to transfer the patient to a stretcher.

"Rosemary, can we put him in the ICU?" Hugh asked her. He took his mask off. "Not that I expect he'll be a problem, but it might be safer . . ."

"We don't have a bed there, Mr. Kirkwall, I'm sorry," replied Rosemary. "The last one was taken this evening, and I don't have anyone well enough to transfer out."

"That's all right," said Hugh. "He's actually quite stable now, and he can go back to his room. Right, Anna?"

At that moment Anna was taking the patient's endotracheal tube out, and Robertson Kelso struggled and bucked. Hugh had to repeat his question.

"Rosemary doesn't have a bed in the ICU, Anna, so I said he could go back to his room, if that's all right with you."

"Yes, he's all right," she said, cleaning the mucus and saliva off Kelso's nose and face with a piece of toweling. She didn't look at Hugh. "His pressure's back to normal, Rosemary, and he doesn't really need to be in the ICU. He can go back to his room."

"There's somebody in the waiting room," said one of the aides to Mr. Kirkwall as the stretcher bearing Kelso trundled along the silent corridors of the hospital. "I think it's Mr. Kelso's wife."

"I'll talk to her," said Hugh distractedly. He was thinking about how he would dictate his operation note so that it wouldn't sound as if he had made a major error during the operation. When a tie came off an artery, as he knew perfectly well, it usually meant that it hadn't been applied correctly in the first place. Maybe it was the effects of the alcohol wearing off, but he was beginning to feel a sense of overwhelming gloom about this case. He knew that it wasn't over, although the patient was all right now. Dr. Shah would surely make as much trouble as possible, and start up his witch-hunt again. Hugh's lips tightened; the entire practice of medicine in Scotland was being polluted by these foreigners, who didn't know the traditions and didn't understand how things were done here. And on top of that, thought Hugh, Shah is a treacherous bastard—a man who couldn't be trusted with the correct time.

Hugh walked alongside the stretcher, the IVs clanking against the poles as it rattled along. He was still thinking about Shah when they turned the corner and rolled the gurney into the room Kelso had been assigned.

"One, two, three!" said Anna, and on the count of three, Hugh, Rosemary, and the two aides each took a corner of the bottom sheet and lifted Kelso from the stretcher to the bed in one easy move.

Anna transferred the IV bags to the pole by the bed. "Do you want to keep both IVs open?" she asked Hugh. When Kelso had his hemorrhage in the operating theatre, she had correctly put in a second wide-bore cannula into Kelso's other arm to provide additional access for intravenous fluids.

"Yes," said Hugh, still thinking about Dr. Shah.

"He's got Ringer's lactate running in one, and saline in the other," said Anna to the night nurse who was going to be taking care of him. As she spoke, she adjusted the flow to the minimum rate. "We'll leave it at a keep-open rate for now," she said. "We gave him almost two liters during his operation." She turned to Hugh. "I have to go now," she said. "I have a respirator patient in the ICU to see. Kelso's fine." She smiled reassuringly at Hugh, then turned and walked back down the corridor to the ICU. There were four patients there, all very sick, and the nurses were being kept as busy as if it had its full complement of six. Anna's respirator patient was in serious condition, and she put everything else out of her mind until he was stabilized, which took her almost an hour.

When she finished with him, she walked back toward Kelso's room, nagged by a thought at the back of her tired mind that something strange had happened that evening, something which didn't ring right. However, she didn't realize what it was until much later; but by then there was nothing she could do about it.

After leaving Kelso, Hugh walked along the quiet corridor to the waiting room, where he found Irene Kelso, Robertson's wife, sitting waiting alone in a chair, hands folded in her lap. Hugh knew about her, as did almost everyone else in Perth, yet he was still shocked by her appearance. Irene was still a young woman, probably in her early to mid-thirties, but she had the typical appearance of a battered wife: the nose, flattened from repeated breaking, the facial scars, and worst of all, the blank, expressionless look that often accompanies years of brutal abuse.

"How is he?" she asked in a dull voice. One of Irene's gray eyes didn't focus properly, and Hugh, full of compassion for the woman, wondered what vicious act had caused that, and guessed that it was probably an orbital fracture that hadn't healed properly.

"He's fine," replied Hugh, wondering if there was anything he could do for her. "His appendix was almost burst; we got it just in time." They looked at each other, and even though they had never met before, the dreadful unspoken message passed through the air between them: It would have been better for everyone if it *had* burst, and Robertson Kelso had died of it.

"When can I see him?"

"He's back in his room," said Hugh. "He's still asleep, but you can go up anytime." He looked at her, full of sympathy. "I'll take you there, if you want," he said. "Come on."

He took her arm and walked her back along the corridor and upstairs to Kelso's room in the private section. The room was almost dark, lit only by a dim light above the bed. Kelso was still asleep; his breathing was slow and regular.

Hugh pulled a chair up for Irene. "Can I get you anything?" he asked. "A cup of tea or something?"

Irene shook her head. "Thank you," she said simply, and sat down, very slowly, her eyes fixed on the prone form of her sleeping husband.

Hugh didn't check the orders that Anna had written; he hardly ever did, because she knew as well as he did what was best for postoperative patients, and she was very reliable. Also Hugh was feeling a powerful and increasing urge to get out of the hospital and to go home. Not that home was a particularly welcoming place these days. Frances had left him a year before, and he'd not been able to get over it. Before that event, Hugh had taken an occasional drink, like everyone else, but of course never when he was on call. After Frances had gone, he drank to get rid of the misery and loneliness. It didn't really help, but nothing else did, either. "Frances, oh, Frances," he would say out loud in his wretchedness. "How could you have done that?" His friends had talked to him, wanted him to take time off, go away somewhere, find another woman, but he couldn't do it. He kept on drinking, to the point where most of his friends got discouraged and left him to his own devices.

"He's trying to destroy himself," Sandy Michie said. Maybe he was. To Hugh, it certainly felt as if his life was over, and now he was just going through the motions, waiting to die. Frances had left quite suddenly, unexpectedly, leaving a little note; he'd kept it and still had it somewhere. Hugh shivered for a second. There was no point in going back over all that. Of course, it didn't make sense to keep on living in that big old house by himself, especially as he wasn't interested in having anyone else live there with him. And with a frightening sense of finality, he knew there never would be.

One of the few good things about living alone, Hugh thought as he came into the silent, empty house, was that there was nobody he had to hide his whisky from. He found the bottle of Glen Grant where he'd left it; thank God it was still about a third full. For some reason, when he was at home, he drank Glen Grant, whereas when he went to a bar he drank Macallan, although the time had long passed since he could taste the difference. He poured himself half a tumblerful and, for the first time in hours, he sat down and was able to relax. He thought of turning on the TV, but decided not to, and just sat there in the darkness, nursing his drink, feeling its familiar, warming fire in his throat when he took a sip. He thought about Frances. He couldn't help it. He felt it in his stomach, that hollow, awful emptiness. Even the *house* missed her lively presence, he was sure of it, missed her step on the floor, missed those red curls bobbing on that pretty, impulsive head . . . It was just too painful to think about her, so he went back to the kitchen and poured the rest of the Glen Grant into his tumbler, drank it, and went to bed. But his sleep was fitful, and he tossed and turned until the gray morning light made pale shadows on the ceiling, and started to spread hesitantly into his room.

When he got up, the first thing he did was brush his teeth to banish the bottom-of-the-parrot's-cage taste in his mouth, then he dressed and got ready to leave for the hospital. It was a few minutes before seven o'clock when he walked in through the doctors' entrance. Unexpectedly, he was feeling more confident today than he had for a long time, maybe because last night he'd got away with what could have been a disaster. As one of his surgical teachers had told him long ago, *better lucky than smart.* But for whatever reason, his step was light, and he felt like the old Hugh Kirkwall, who had once been the best surgeon in Perth, the toast of the town, and the heartthrob of the area.

He went up the stairs two at a time, to the fourth floor where the private patients were housed. There was no one at the nurses' station, so he walked quickly along the corridor to Robertson Kelso's room. He paused for a moment outside the door, then knocked perfunctorily, opened the door, and walked in. The room was in darkness, and he walked over to the window and pulled the curtains, letting the early morning light into the room. Kelso was still asleep, on his back, his mouth a little open.

"Wake up, Kelso!" said Hugh grimly in a voice pitched just loud enough to rouse him.

There was no answer.

Hugh approached the bed, and a sudden awful fear grabbed at him. Kelso was lying very still, and didn't seem to be breathing. Hugh, his own heart racing fit to explode, reached for Kelso's wrist, feeling for his pulse. The wrist was cold, and there was no pulse.

Robertson Kelso was dead.

Chapter 4

At eight o'clock that morning, Jean Montrose was standing in her kitchen, waiting for the kettle to boil. She'd wakened her two daughters, Fiona and Lisbie, ten minutes before, and they had appeared from their basement bedrooms in various stages of deshabille. Mrs. Findlay, Jean's mother, who was still recuperating from a fractured hip, didn't usually get up until about ten; sometimes she spent the entire day in bed.

The phone rang. Here we go, Jean thought, the day's started.

She picked it up. But it wasn't a patient, or Eleanor, but Detective Inspector Douglas Niven, of the Tayside Police, and from the metallic sound of his voice, she knew that he was using his radio telephone.

"Jean? I'm up at the hospital," he said, his soft Glasgow accent strong on him. "One of your patients died, Robertson Kelso . . ."

Horrified, Jean put a hand up to her mouth. "He *died*? But . . ."

"Aye. They found him this morning. Jean, the situation's actually a bit complicated . . . The man had his appendix removed last night, I'm sure you know that already. We wouldn't be normally involved, but it's become a coroner's case, as the death occurred within forty-eight hours of a general anesthetic being given." Douglas hesitated, and his voice lacked its usual assuredness. "And, in addition, one of the emergency doctors, a Dr. . . ." Douglas paused while he looked again at the paper in his hand, "Dr. Ramashandra Shah, called us. He *insisted* that the police come up to the hospital and investigate. . . ."

Douglas's voice became muffled for a moment; Jean assumed he was talking to someone next to him. Then he came back. "Yes, I'm sorry, Jean . . . Dr. Shah told me that criminal negligence was involved, and that the surgeon who did the operation was intoxicated at the time."

"Oh, my goodness," said Jean, appalled. "Mr. Kirkwall phoned me before he started the operation, and he sounded all right to me . . . Oh, dear, that's just terrible." Jean paused, thinking of the implications. "How is Irene taking it? His wife?" she asked.

"Mrs. Kelso was not with him at the time," replied Doug. "She went home after staying with him for a while. The hospital phoned her, and she's on her way in."

Jean was silent for a moment, thinking. Then she said in a very quiet voice, "Douglas, do you think that this could have been anything else, besides an accident? I mean . . ."

"Well, Jean, I'm standing here in the room looking at him, and I don't see any knives sticking out of his chest, if that's what you mean," replied Douglas. He went on in a quieter voice, "which is not to say that quite a few people won't be happy to see the death notice in the *Courier*."

"Oh, my goodness," said Jean, her mind racing. "Douglas, what are you going to do?"

"I'll talk to the people who were involved in the operation. If it seems that there was criminal negligence, we'll have to follow that up, but my guess is that it'll turn out to be just one of those things that happens in hospitals from time to time. Then we'll report that to the coroner."

Fiona put a cup of tea in front of Jean, who smiled a distracted thank-you. Fiona hung around, watching her mother's face, having guessed whom Jean was talking to.

"Jean . . ." Doug's voice took on a slightly hesitant tone, and Jean sighed to herself. She knew what was coming.

"Jean, you know I'm not really familiar with all this medical stuff, and I'm going to need some help. Now, Robertson Kelso was your patient, and so to some extent it's your responsibility. . . ."

"No," said Jean firmly. "Absolutely not. Douglas Niven, I've told you I'm not getting mixed up in your cases anymore, and just the fact that Robertson Kelso was a patient of mine doesn't change my decision. Now, was there anything else?"

"Well, can I come and talk to you about it?"

There was an almost comical edge of desperation in Doug's voice.

"Douglas, you know perfectly well that you're welcome here anytime . . ."

"And that goes for me, too," said Fiona, loudly enough to be heard at the other end. Fiona had a long-standing infatuation with Douglas, in spite of the fact that he was a happily married man with a young son.

Jean put down the phone slowly, all kinds of thoughts passing through her mind. Then she looked at the clock. "My goodness," she said to Lisbie and Fiona. "If you two don't hurry up, you'll both be late for work."

Twenty minutes later, Jean got into her little red Renault and headed off down the hill to the surgery, trying to concentrate on the day ahead, but her mind kept coming back to Robertson Kelso. That horrible man . . . It amazed her to think that he had never been put in jail, or even, for that matter, taken to court, although his activities were notorious. Kelso was a wife beater who also brutally ill-treated his son. He also had a long history of getting into trouble with women, going back to the time when he was just the spoiled teenage son of old Huntly Kelso, one of the most powerful and influential men in Perth. Huntly had been a forthright, honest, self-made businessman who, at the time he died, owned a big fish-processing plant and a number of other related businesses which Robertson had inherited some years ago. But when his son Robertson took over, he quickly developed a bad reputation because of the sharp and ruthless way he did business, and although he had done well financially and his empire kept on growing, he was feared and hated by more than a few unfortunate people who had been unwise enough to cross him.

Jean stopped off for petrol at the Shell station on the Dunkeld Road, and went into the station to pay for it with her credit card. John Gallacher, the manager, who had known Jean for years, greeted her from behind his desk. John was a big, grizzled man, a former SAS sergeant with huge, tattooed arms. Several black-and-white military photos pinned to the wall attested to his contribution to the Falklands victory. One smiling photo, taken years before, showed him with his wife, both in uniform; she had been an army nurse when they met.

John grinned at Jean, held out his hand for her credit card, and looked out at her car. "If you ever want to sell your Renault, Dr. Montrose," he said, "I'd like to buy it. My nephew needs a car, but he can't afford a good one yet." He paused, then said, "Oh, I didn't mean . . ."

"That's all right, John," said Jean, laughing. She made her mind up that instant. "I've decided it's time I got a new one. Another Renault, or maybe a Vauxhall. What do you think?"

They discussed the pros and cons of the different models, and Jean promised to give him first refusal on her Renault.

"Did you hear about Robertson Kelso?" he

asked her as she put her receipt in her handbag before leaving.

Jean nodded, surprised that the news had got out so quickly, but then she remembered that John's wife worked up at the hospital. Jean's expression made it clear that she wasn't going to discuss the matter.

"It's a good riddance," said the usually cheerful John. The grimness of his tone showed how strongly he felt. "It's a pity he died like that," he went on, coming around to open the door for Jean. "That man didn't deserve to die a natural death."

As soon as Dr. Shah heard the news of Robertson Kelso's death, he swung into action. His first call was to the police, then he phoned Sandy Michie, the hospital administrator, at home, to report the matter. But Michie resisted Shah's pressure to come in and immediately suspend Hugh Kirkwall's hospital privileges. He knew from long experience that if he stayed out of the way and waited long enough, most problems would resolve themselves. When he did eventually show up, he found Dr. Shah and Detective Inspector Douglas Niven, flanked by the large and imposing figure of Constable Jamieson, Doug's assistant, waiting outside his office.

"Yes, gentlemen, please come in," said Mr. Michie, resignedly unlocking the door. They followed him in. It was an unimpressive place, with a high, dreary-looking window that obviously had not been cleaned for some time, an old wooden desk, and a number of photographs on the wall showing the last phase of the hospital restorations—a project that had been completed some dozen years before.

Douglas walked in ahead of Dr. Shah, anxious to get early control of this situation, not always an easy thing to do in someone else's office.

"Dr. Shah, if you'll sit here . . . and Jamieson . . ." He pointed at a spot on the carpet in front of the door, and Jamieson resignedly took up his position there. "Yes, Mr. Michie, if you'd care to sit down at your desk," he went on. Sandy Michie looked a little astonished, as he was already in the process of sitting down in his chair, but he said nothing and merely passed the flat of his hand over the shiny dome of his head. Dr. Shah, in his submissive-appearing way, sat down in the chair Doug had indicated. He put his knees modestly and tightly together, and clasped his hands in his lap.

Doug opened his mouth, but Sandy Michie got in ahead of him.

"And why are you here, Inspector?" he asked mildly.

"A call was put in to headquarters at two minutes after eight this morning," said Douglas in his heavy, official voice. He was annoyed to be answering questions rather than asking them. "The caller reported that a death had occurred in the hospital this morning, and that the circumstances were suspicious. The caller also said that the deceased was Mr. Robertson Kelso. *The* Mr. Robertson Kelso."

"And who might that caller have been?" asked Sandy, glowering suspiciously at Dr. Shah.

"The caller did not identify himself," replied Doug, carefully avoiding looking at Dr. Shah. "But the operator thought he had a foreign accent, possibly an Indian or a Paki ... stani." Doug just remembered to finish the word.

They both looked at Dr. Shah, who made no move or sound to confirm or deny his involvement.

"Actually, it doesn't really matter who phoned," Douglas went on. "What I do want to know is if there was any actual grounds for such a phone call."

"Mr. Kelso was certainly a patient here," said Michie, after a careful pause. "And I understand that he did indeed pass away in the early hours of this morning."

"After an operation for appendicitis, carried out by Mr. Hugh Kirkwall," murmured Dr. Shah.

"Well, that makes it an automatic coroner's case, doesn't it, Inspector?" asked Mr. Michie.

Doug nodded. "So why were we called?" This time he looked straight at Dr. Shah.

"Presumably, because foul play was suspected," replied Shah. He saw that Michie was about to say something, and went on quickly, "And the hospital bylaws state, and I quote, "if any hospital employee suspects that a patient has been the victim of assault *or any other criminal action*, the matter must be reported immediately to the employee's supervisor and to the police.' "

"And why do you think there might be criminal

action involved in this case?" asked Doug, a hint of sarcasm in his voice. "Did you find a knife sticking out of his chest, or a bullet in his head?" Doug's voice rose a fraction. "There certainly wasn't anything like that when I examined the body. So, Dr. Shah, what makes you think that this was any more than an unfortunate postoperative death, something that could occur without criminal action whatsoever, in any hospital?"

"Several things come to mind, Inspector," replied Shah, quite unruffled. "Mr. Robertson Kelso was a relatively young man, in otherwise perfect health. He had no history of heart disease or other potentially fatal condition. He underwent a comparatively minor appendix operation, and was found dead by the surgeon who operated on him."

"Is that all?" asked Doug, annoyed. "Because if it is . . ."

"Not at all," said Shah smoothly. "I'm sorry to have to tell you this, particularly in front of the hospital administrator, but at the time of the operation Mr. Kirkwall was the worse for drink."

"We can certainly get evaluations of Mr. Kirkwall's condition from the nurses and others who were working with him," said Douglas coldly, thinking that Dr. Shah was clearly motivated by more than an honest search for truth. Even Doug, who had no interest in the inner workings of the hospital, had heard comments about Shah's disruptive ambitions. And now, every instinct warned Doug not to allow himself to get sucked into this situation, let alone help Shah achieve his goals. He squared his shoulders and spoke to Shah. "Sir, is there any other *valid* reason that would make you think Mr. Kirkwall might be involved in Kelso's death?"

Shah nodded, very emphatically. "Yes, sir, indeed," he said. "A most valid reason, in fact, *the most* important reason to suspect that Mr. Kelso did not die accidentally." He looked around at them and sat up very straight, primly gratified to have the full attention of the others, and his eyes glittered with intensity. "About a year ago," he said, "as many people in Perth are aware, Mr. Robertson Kelso very boldly ran off with Mr. Kirkwall's wife, Frances."

Chapter 5

Shah's comment was followed by a long, astonished silence.

"I didn't know that," said Doug, caught off guard.

"I have heard some rumors of that sort," said Sandy, sounding really annoyed now. "But as far as I'm concerned, that's all they were. Rumors." He turned brusquely toward Shah. "Do you *know* that? Or are you simply repeating those ... damaging allegations about one of your colleagues?"

"Most regrettably, it is common knowledge, sir," said Shah, spreading his hands, taking no responsibility for what people chose to say.

"You mentioned that Mr. Kirkwall was the worse for drink," said Michie. "If that was so, why did you let him even see the patient?" Michie rubbed the bald dome of his head. Like many others at the hospital, he didn't trust Dr. Shah, and didn't like the sneaky way he attacked other doctors—particularly Hugh Kirkwall. Nor did he like his attitude, his persistence, and his self-serving readiness to cause trouble.

"His intoxication was not apparent at the time he first saw Mr. Kelso, sir," Shah replied in that falsely humble, high-pitched voice that grated so much on Sandy Michie's nerves. "And, in any case, I am not responsible for policing my colleagues. But it was very apparent when I, in the presence of Nurse Gallacher, observed him in the operating theatre."

"And what were the two of you doing in the operating theatre, if you didn't think there was a problem?"

"I am unable to speak for Mrs. Gallacher, of course," replied Shah, smooth as a silk turban. "But I was there as a result of my interest in the diagnosis on Mr. Kelso, who, as you recall, I had been the first to see in the emergency room."

"Did you *know* Mr. Kelso?" Michie looked at Shah with a certain scepticism.

"Not personally. And with respect, sir, I think we are not sticking to the question at hand. And that question is how to deal with this catastrophe and how we can best to protect other patients from similar misfortune."

"Well," said Michie, making a dismissive gesture with his hand, "I'm sure that if we let all this hubbub die down, everything will come back to normal. For one thing, at this time we don't even know the cause of Kelso's death."

"Oh, but, sir, I think we do." Shah clasped his hands together. "The patient had an uncontrolled hemorrhage during the operation, and Mr. Kirkwall refused to order the necessary blood replacement, even after it had been suggested by the anesthetist. Mr. Kelso died as a result of that mistreatment."

Doug moved restlessly on his chair. He was now deep into unfamiliar territory, and wished that Jean Montrose were there to explain this complicated medical stuff to him.

"Well, I'm not a doctor, and I can't make any kind of judgment on that," said Michie curtly. "I'll have to talk to the anesthetist. . . ." He looked at the papers on his desk. "That was Anna McKenzie, according to the on-call schedule. Yes. I also have here the names of the nurses who helped him. Meanwhile . . ." Michie stood up. "Thanks for your help, Dr. Shah. I'll call you if I need any more information on this sorry business." He glanced at Doug. "Unless, of course, Inspector Niven has any further questions for you."

"Not right now," said Doug. "But I certainly will in the near future, so please remain available."

"Of course, sir." Shah took a business card from his wallet and handed it to Doug. "My home telephone number is there, Inspector. Please to call me at any time."

Without looking at Shah, Doug nodded and put the card away.

Dr. Shah turned to address Michie. "There will be a great deal of anxiety among the hospital staff and among the townspeople, sir," he went on, making no move to stand up or leave. "Everyone knows about the unfortunate drinking problem of

Mr. Kirkwall, and as a result, there has already been a serious loss of public confidence in this hospital, because so far no steps have been taken to correct the problem. And now ..." Dr. Shah spread his hands wide. "Now, unless immediate action is taken, we can no doubt expect this tragedy to come to the attention of national authorities, and of course the press and television, which I fear will be less than friendly."

"As of this moment," said Sandy, glowering, "I forbid anyone connected with this hospital to discuss the matter with the press or any other branch of the media, and I'll make a general announcement to that effect. And of course that includes you, Dr. Shah." He stared hard at Dr. Shah, who in the past had been known to ignore orders, then plead that his limited understanding of English had been the cause. "Do you understand what I'm saying, Dr. Shah?"

"In addition, I have no doubt that numerous individuals would desire the police to investigate this tragedy," replied Shah, ignoring the question and speaking a little faster, and still wearing that infuriatingly bogus expression of total frankness. "And I certainly was not surprised to see them arrive here."

"Has anyone heard from Mrs. Kirkwall?" asked Doug unexpectedly. "Does she still live in Perth?"

There was a brief silence, broken by a deep harrumph from Jamieson, who was still standing near the door, his presence until now barely registering with the others. "I believe she now lives with her parents," said Jamieson, after getting visual permission from Doug to speak. "In Aviemore or thereabouts."

Again there was a brief silence, broken this time by Sandy Michie. "Frances Kirkwall was a very good woman," he said defensively, as if challenging the others to contradict him. "Everybody liked her here. She was very popular in the community, and she was certainly the best bacteriologist we ever had working here in the hospital. Until . . . That man seems to have had uncanny powers over women," he went on musingly, obviously referring to Kelso. "He'd mark out his target, apparently sweep them off their feet; young and old and in between, but they soon found out what he was really like."

Shah didn't even hear what Michie was saying, he was so anxious to get some official action going against Hugh Kirkwall. "Please, gentlemen," he said, placing his palms together, "could we return to the topic that has brought us here? At present, Mr. Kirkwall is a danger to the community, and I really must insist that . . ."

"How did Mrs. Kelso react to all this . . . philandering?" Douglas asked Michie, deliberately ignoring the agitated Shah.

"She was terrified of him," replied Michie, happy to assist Doug in putting Shah in his place. "Haven't you seen her face? She's a battered wife, poor woman, although she's never brought any charges, not that I know of. When he'd go off with one of his new women, she'd just stay home up in that big house with her son, probably glad that he wasn't around."

Shah stood up angrily, but before he could say anything, Michie addressed him. "To answer your question, Dr. Shah, I've decided not to do anything about Mr. Kirkwall's hospital privileges, certainly not until after we've had an investigation of the Kelso case," he said, his voice bland. "In this country, as I'm sure you're aware, we still hold to the precept of *innocent until proven guilty*. Of course, if it turns out that negligence on Mr. Kirkwall's part was a factor in Kelso's death, *then* I will take whatever measures are appropriate." Not usually a confrontational man, Michie now stood up and stared at Shah. "And now, Dr. Shah," he said, knowing that tact would be wasted, "I don't believe there's any need to keep you here any longer."

"Very good, sir," said Shah, his expression becoming masklike. "I hope you will not regret this, at a crucial time when decisive action is needed."

But as he left, Dr. Shah did not feel in the least defeated. This was only the first skirmish of the war, and he had plenty more ammunition. And when Michie was ultimately forced to take Kirkwall's hospital privileges away from him, he, Shah, would make sure that Kirkwall never got them back.

Chapter 6

"Mum, can I bring May home for supper tomorrow?" Lisbie was setting the table in the dining room, Jean was making dinner in the kitchen, and Fiona was in the doorway of the kitchen, from which vantage point she could see both her mother and her sister. The open hatch between the two rooms allowed them all to communicate, even if they didn't always see each other.

"Oh, please!" Fiona rolled her eyes. "Why can't Lisbie have any normal friends?" she asked her mother. "We shouldn't have to put up with . . ."

"Of course you can, Lisbie," interrupted Jean, throwing a warning glance at Fiona. "It'll be lovely to see her."

"Lovely!" Moving out of Lisbie's line of sight, Fiona made exaggerated twitching movements, and Jean frowned reprovingly.

Steven often said that Lisbie was a rescuer of dying dogs, and it was true that she had a soft spot for any creature that had been hurt or incapacitated in any way. From the time she was a little girl, birds with broken wings, baby rabbits, or fledglings that had fallen out of their nests, made regular appearances in the Montrose household, to be tenderly nursed in cotton-wool nests by Lisbie. Once in a while her ministrations were successful enough so the animal could be returned to the wild, or at least to the nearest available approximation, the Montroses' small but tidy back garden.

Lisbie had first met May Gallacher a few months before, at their church, St. John's, where Lisbie was a member of the choir. After the morning service the choir usually met for coffee in the vestry, and occasionally Mr. Cattanach, the new minister, would invite other parishioners in to join them. On this occasion, Mr. Cattanach had invited several people, including May and her mother. May was a pretty girl, with blond hair and big blue eyes, about sixteen years old. But it didn't take long to see that there was a vacancy in her look, and her eyes moved around in a way that wasn't quite normal. Lisbie, chatting with a fellow choir member at the time, smiled at May when she walked past, with her mother holding her by the arm, on their way to the trestle table where the tea and coffee and biscuits had been set out. A minute later there was a crash, a cup and saucer went flying, and someone screamed. Lisbie turned to see May on the floor, twitching in a terrifying way, her mother already down on her knees to help her. She took something out of her purse and pushed it between May's teeth. "It's an epileptic attack," she said to Lisbie, who had instantly come

over to help. "She gets them from time to time."
She smiled at Lisbie's concerned face. "It'll be over
in a minute."

Lisbie took a small pile of paper napkins from
the table and placed them under May's head, and
stayed with her until she opened her eyes and
stared around. Most of the choir had backed off
and were keeping a wary eye on them from near
the door. Mr. Cattanach, who had been standing
on the entrance steps bidding farewell to his parishioners, came in at that point and hurried over
when he saw May on the floor. "Oh, my goodness, Rosemary, whatever happened? Did May
fall?"

May's mother explained. Soon after, May was
able to sit up, and a few moments later she struggled to her feet. Mr. Cattanach quickly brought
over a chair, and sat her down in it. Lisbie talked
quietly to May, brought her a cup of water, and
held it for her to drink. Soon May had recovered
enough to get up and go home with her mother.
Since that incident, Lisbie had made a point of
talking to them after church. She even tried to get
May to sing with them, but although she had a
good enough voice, she'd lose track of what they
were singing and stare mutely up at the high
Gothic ceiling of the church, her eyes searching
vaguely for something that sadly wasn't there.

"May had a bad accident a year ago," her
mother explained to Lisbie one Sunday. "She was
all right before that."

Later, Lisbie learned that before her accident,

May had done a three-month summer internship with an aquaculture company near Perth, and had hoped to come back a year or two later as a trainee manager. However, that, like her other dreams, was gone. May couldn't go to school or talk about boys or play sports, so most of her friends had gradually drifted off. Now May spent most of her time at an adult day-care centre or at home watching television. Lisbie's tender heart was touched, and every so often she'd invite May to the Montrose house for dinner or Sunday lunch. And, of course, Jean and Steven, who felt sorry for May and her parents, were happy to welcome her into their home. Even Fiona, though she pretended to object to May's presence, was as kind to her as any of them.

Lisbie was solemnly promising to make dinner the next day, but everyone laughed so loudly that finally she left in a huff, and stamped down the stairs to her room in the basement, slamming the door. Lisbie's culinary abilities were legendary by their absence, whereas Fiona, with no apparent effort, could put together a delicious meal in minutes from whatever happened to be in the refrigerator and the larder.

The telephone rang, and Fiona, who was nearest, answered it. "It's for you, Mum," she said, holding the receiver until Jean took it.

"Yes, hello, Jean? Dr. Montrose?"

It took Jean a moment to recognize Hugh Kirkwall's voice. It was high-pitched, as if he had reached some kind of breaking point and his voice no longer did what it was told to do.

"Yes, Hugh. What can I do for you?" Alarmed at his tone, Jean spoke softly and slowly, to give him time to collect himself.

"Jean ... Listen, I'm really embarrassed, but quite honestly, I don't know what to do."

"Do? About what?"

"Well, it's about Kelso, Robertson Kelso. I think they're trying to make out that I killed him. On purpose."

"Who is, Hugh?" Soundlessly, Jean pointed at the covered dish on the countertop, and signaled to Fiona to put it in the oven.

"Well, the police, for one, and the people at the hospital, especially Dr. Shah. You know him, don't you?"

Jean had met Shah, but knew him more by reputation. She was aware that nobody seemed to like him very much, and in her own personal experience with him, he'd seemed aloof and disdainful.

"But why on earth would they want to do that?"

"Jean, I don't think I should talk about this over the phone." He hesitated. "May I come over to see you?"

"Yes, of course," replied Jean, looking at the clock. She knew about Hugh's domestic circumstances, and her motherly instinct came to the surface. "Hugh, have you had dinner?"

"Oh, Mum, for heavens' sake!" mouthed Fiona.

As usual, she was listening to the conversation and glowered at her mother.

"Actually, I hadn't even thought about dinner," replied Hugh, "but I wouldn't dream of disturbing your evening meal. . . ."

"You won't be disturbing anything," replied Jean. "We'll be starting in about an hour, so come anytime before then."

"Mum!" said Fiona as soon as the phone was back on the hook. "Why did you invite him? We don't even know him."

"*I* know him," replied Jean calmly. "I've known him for a long time. He's always been very nice to me, and right now he's a very sad and unhappy man, so I thought it would be a pleasant change for him. He lives by himself, and it must be very boring to eat alone all the time."

"I wouldn't mind that one bit," said Fiona glumly. She looked down the stairs toward Lisbie's room. "Set another place, please, Lisbie," she called out in a loud, put-upon tone.

"You don't need to shout, dear," said Jean, but already her mind was elsewhere, thinking about Hugh and his pretty, clever wife, Frances, whom Jean had known and liked a lot. Then Jean's mind turned to that evil man, Robertson Kelso, and she felt a sense of apprehension rising around her like a malignant tide. His sins had not died with him, she realized, but would continue to cause as much suffering, as much pain, as when he was alive.

*　　*　　*

Douglas Niven was feeling uncomfortable about the situation at the hospital. For one thing, it was an unfamiliar place, a world of its own with different customs and ways of doing things that were quite alien to him.

But here he was, and so he had to make the best of it.

From the beginning, it was difficult.

"I'd like to have a room I can use for interviewing," he asked Sandy Michie.

Sandy, already very put out by the situation, and at having the police investigating a case inside his hospital, was not in a mood to cooperate. "I'm sorry, Inspector," he said, "but this is a hospital, not a conference centre. We don't have any spare offices."

Douglas had no problems dealing with this kind of attitude. Not only was he used to it, but he actually enjoyed it, because he nearly always won. As he liked to tell Jamieson, that first win is important, because it gives an advantage you can consolidate and build upon.

"Very well, then, Mr. Michie," he said in his briskly official tone, "we'll do our interviewing down at headquarters, if that's really what you wish. It may take some time, and of course your personnel will probably have to wait there awhile. I don't suppose they'll be happy about that, and I don't suppose your board will be delighted when they hear about all the waste of time and money involved. But, of course, Mr. Michie, that's your decision."

Somehow, a vacant room was found, an office normally used by the day nursing supervisor, at present on vacation. There was a desk, a phone, lots of photos and illustrations of cats and puppies, and two chairs, each with a well-stuffed homemade cushion featuring a large gros-point pink rose.

Douglas, feeling insecure and sour, looked at the gold-framed family photo on the desk. It showed a comfortable-looking, smiling woman, no doubt the supervisor herself, with a shorter, thinner man with a bald head and a harassed expression, and two nondescript adolescent children, both obviously fighting losing battles with the dermatological hazards of puberty.

"You see, Jamieson," said Doug, his voice caustic, pointing at the photo, "a typical Perth domestic scene. She's fat and happy, he's a wreck, ready for the knacker's yard. That's what women can do to you."

"It didn't happen to you," retorted Jamieson. "And I don't think you'd repeat what you just said in front of Mrs. Niven, either."

Doug's eyebrows went up, surprised at the speed and accuracy of Jamieson's repartee, then down again. He put a sheet of paper on the desk, wrote for a few moments, then stared at the list. "Okay, let's see, now . . . We have several people from the hospital that we need to talk to. For a start, there's Mr. Hugh Kirkwall, of course, and Dr. Anna McKenzie, who gave the anesthesia. Then we have the night supervisor, Mrs. Gallacher . . . Anybody else?"

"Well, there's Dr. Shah, and of course Mrs. Kelso."

Doug looked sharply at Jamieson, then wrote on the paper. "Right. But Mrs. Kelso doesn't work here, so we'll talk to her later. As for Dr. Shah . . . Yes, I suppose we'll have to talk to him again. Even though we've heard his story once already."

Jamieson could hear the reluctance in his boss's voice. "Nobody likes him much," he observed.

Doug shrugged. "This isn't a popularity contest. Who do you think we should start with?"

"Mr. Kirkwall, I suppose. So far, he seems to be the main character in this case, and we haven't spoken to him yet."

"That's a very good reason to put him last, Jamieson," said Douglas, taking on a didactic tone that Jamieson had learned to hate.

With an expression that held both resignation and annoyance, Jamieson stared at Doug and said, almost under his breath, "You'd have made some objection, whoever I suggested."

Doug ignored the words; he may not even have heard them, because in his mind, the flow of information and intelligence between himself and Jamieson went only in one direction.

"When you have a suspect, Jamieson, and I'm talking about a situation like this one"—he waved a hand vaguely to include the hospital and all its inhabitants—"the more you can find out about that person, the better. If you talk with the others first, you can get, like, a composite picture of the man you're after, each person giving you a different perspective. Then, when you interview the suspect in person, you have a better idea of the kind of questions you need to ask."

Doug's wise reflections didn't seem to be finding their mark, however. Jamieson was looking around the office with a distracted look, and said, "I was trying to remember what the name Caie made me think of."

"Caie?"

"Aye. Doris. The nurse who was in the emergency room when Kelso came in. Isn't she on your list?"

Doug wrote the name down, guessing at the spelling—he didn't want to ask Jamieson. That was a funny kind of name, *Caie*, he thought. Scottish enough, but he wondered which part of the country it came from.

"What about her?"

"Not her. Do you remember that business with an *Albert* Caie, about a couple of years ago? It was in the papers, just a wee paragraph, and it appeared just once, because Kelso said it was libelous, and he'd sue the paper if they printed one more word about it."

Douglas, bemused, shook his head. Jamieson, whom Douglas tolerantly put in the category of cerebrally challenged, sometimes put him to shame with his knowledge of local people and events. But of course, thought Doug, immediately coming to his own defense, unlike him, Jamieson was a local Perth lad who knew all these people from birth, and thus had a kind of vested, genetically linked interest in following up news items that to Douglas were not of any particular importance. "So what was the story about Albert Caie?"

Jamieson, in the unusual position of having Douglas's full attention, sat down and annoyingly proceeded to take advantage of the situation. He leaned back in his chair, and started the story in a ponderous raconteur's style that immediately set Doug's teeth on edge. Before he could interrupt, there was a knock on the door.

It was Willie Angus, a young man known to both Douglas and Jamieson, latest in the line of the Angus family of undertakers, who in their time had buried a goodly proportion of the citizens of Perth and looked forward gloomily to burying the rest. Willie was a fine-looking lad, with bright, sharp eyes and a thick mane of dark brown hair. He had a passion for his work that had made more than one young woman wonder if he was worth dying for, as nothing else seemed to hold his attention longer than it took to dance a Strathspey. Willie, a recent graduate of the Embalming Academy of Pitfodels, had duly learned the obsequiousness of his trade as part of the curriculum, but it still sat uncomfortably on him.

"Excuse me, Inspector Niven," he said, "but I'd like to have Mr. Kelso's body released to us, in accordance with Mrs. Kelso's instructions. I already asked Mr. Michie, of course, but he said it was now in your hands."

Willie stepped up to the desk, holding out the partially completed form in his outstretched hand.

"It's a coroner's case, my lad," said Doug, without looking up. "And there'll probably be a post-mortem. If you tell Dr. Anderson's office that you're in charge of the burial, they'll let you know when you can pick up the body."

"Mrs. Kelso is very anxious to proceed with the arrangements, sir," said Willie, standing his ground. "The chapel's been booked for a memorial service at the crematorium on Wednesday, and . . ."

"A memorial service! For *Robertson Kelso!*" Douglas looked up, and his voice held contempt and disbelief. "And who do you think might attend such an event, Mr. Willie Angus?"

"All the people who want to be quite certain that he's dead, sir," replied Willie, straight-faced.

Jamieson guffawed loudly until he was abruptly silenced by one of Doug's icy looks.

"And who wants him cremated?" asked Doug. "Would that possibly also be Mrs. Kelso?"

"She's the next of kin, sir, and yes, she is the one who made that decision."

"Very interesting," said Doug. "Did you talk to her personally?"

"Yes, sir. She phoned first thing this morning . . . Actually, the phone was ringing when I came in. I usually get to work before anyone else."

"Loves his job," remarked Doug, looking at the ceiling. "Must be nice, to love your job, don't you think, Jamieson?"

"Yes, sir," replied Jamieson. His voice sounded almost ludicrously morose.

Doug looked up at Willie. "And what time would that have been, Mr. Angus? When Mrs. Kelso phoned you?"

"About eight-thirty," said Willie. "A few minutes after."

"Thank you, Willie. That'll be all for now."

"Mr. Kelso's possessions, sir. Mrs. Kelso would like to have those returned to her as soon as possible."

"It's all being held at present as possible evidence," said Doug, "and will be returned to her in due course." He stood up. "As I just said, Willie Angus, that will be all for now."

Willie stared at him eye to eye for one fighting second, then his embalming school training took over and he beat a respectful retreat.

"A few minutes after eight-thirty," said Doug thoughtfully when the door had closed behind Willie's dark suit. "It was only a quarter after eight or thereabouts when we phoned her with the tragic news, wasn't it?"

"Yes, sir. Exactly a quarter after eight."

"Well, she didn't waste anytime arranging the funeral, did she? Just a matter of overcoming a few seconds of unbearable grief, right, Jamieson?" Reflexively, Doug reached for the pack of cigarettes in his shirt pocket, then remembered that he'd given them up. Months ago. He gazed thoughtfully through Jamieson's solid head. "And she also seems extremely anxious to turn his mortal remains into smoke, too."

"I'd have thought she'd have wanted him cremated *before* he died," observed Jamieson. "Judging from what they say he did to her."

"Let's get on with the interviews," said Douglas, tapping his pen on the plastic veneer of the desk. "We'll start with Dr. Anna McKenzie, because she is probably the one who's least involved." He glanced at his subordinate to see if he'd understood. Then he shrugged and said, "Ask Mr. Michie's secretary. She'll know where to find her."

Jamieson stood up and went off, and a few moments later, Doug heard the paging system calling for Dr. Anna McKenzie. A couple of minutes went by, and she came in with Jamieson, in her surgical garb, looking rather flustered. She was pale-skinned, pretty, with freckles on her cheeks that made her look like a thirty-something teenager. She pulled off her paper cap to reveal blond, rather straggly hair that, freed from the restraints of the cap, seemed to point in all directions at once.

Very politely, Douglas introduced himself, told her that they were doing a routine investigation, and hoped that she could help them.

"I'd like you to think back to yesterday evening, Dr. McKenzie," he said. "At what time did you first see the patient Robertson Kelso?"

Anna looked up at the ceiling and thought for a second. "It must have been about eight o'clock, soon after Mr. Kirkwall had seen him and decided he needed to be operated on."

Doug made a notation on the paper in front of him.

"Did you know the patient?"

"No. But I'd heard about him."

"And Mr. Kirkwall, how long have you known him?"

"I've just been in Perth for a year," replied Anna, in what sounded to Doug like a cautious tone.

Doug waited for a moment, then said in an encouraging voice, "So you've known him for about a year?"

"Yes. Actually, I met him just around the time when . . ." Anna hesitated, and looked at them. She had big blue eyes, and the dark eyelashes and thin line of mascara made them look even bigger.

"When?" prompted Doug.

"When he was having his . . . domestic problems," said Anna. She looked at the floor, then back up at Doug. "I suppose you know about that."

"A little," replied Doug, in a tone which indicated that he knew much more than she ever would.

"When I first came, everybody told me how nice he was, and that he was the best surgeon in Perth," said Anna, sounding a bit defensive.

"And would you say that was your own personal experience, working with him, Dr. McKenzie?"

"Yes it was." Anna moved on the chair, and her voice was strong. "He's a good colleague, and he was very nice to me, as a newcomer. And he's technically very competent, a good diagnostician, and he's good to his patients. They all love him."

"Dr. McKenzie," said Doug, in his confidential I-need-your-help voice, "we know about the problems that Mr. Kirkwall's been having, and we need to know how much of a part, if any, it played in yesterday's events."

"He does drink too much, of course," said Anna frankly, responding to Doug's manner. "But that's no secret. And he's been known to see patients when he shouldn't. But I can tell you this," she said, and her eyes took on a flashing quality, "I'd rather be operated on by Hugh Kirkwall drunk than any of the others sober. And I can assure you that that goes for most of the staff here." Anna's mouth opened slightly. "I know I shouldn't have said that," she said very quietly. "But it's true."

"Everything you tell us at this point will be kept confidential, Dr. McKenzie," Doug assured her. "All we're trying to do is find out whether Mr. Kelso's death needs to be investigated."

"There was some bleeding during the operation," said Anna. "The patient's blood pressure dropped a bit, but he was all right by the time we finished. I mean, if he'd been in trouble, or even if we'd been concerned about him, then we'd have put him in intensive care, but we all felt he was well enough to go back to his room." Again Anna half remembered something that had disturbed her that night, but she couldn't quite pinpoint what it was.

"So why do you think he died?"

"I can't imagine. Probably heart failure of some kind." Anna seemed uncomfortable, and wouldn't look at either of them. "Sometimes after surgical operations, patients can get cardiac arrhythmias for no apparent reason and die suddenly from them, but as far as we could tell, Kelso was in good physical condition. Very good."

Jamieson, who was taking notes, looked up and sighed. "Cardiac what-was-that?" he asked Anna.

"Arrhythmias." She spelled it out for him. "It means irregularity of the heartbeat."

Douglas, watching her, wondered if she was feeling guilty about Kelso's death, and decided to push it a little. "When a death occurs within twenty-four hours of surgery, isn't that termed an anesthetic death?" he asked.

Anna went pink. "Yes, that is the technical term that's used, but I can tell you there was no problem with the anesthesia. Everything went very smoothly at my end of the table."

"You didn't use any unusual drugs or medications?"

"No. First we used succinylcholine, a short-acting muscle relaxant, then one percent Halothane plus oxygen. If there had been a problem with any of the medications, we'd have found out during the operation."

"Would you mind if we asked another anesthetist to examine the records?"

"Not at all." Anna looked surprised and offended.

Douglas bored in. "To whom do you feel your

prime responsibility is, Dr. McKenzie, to your colleagues, or to the patient?"

"The patient, of course," replied Anna.

Doug got the impression that she was replying reflexively, merely giving a learned response, so he turned the heat up a little.

"Did you think that Mr. Kirkwall was under the influence of alcohol at the time he performed surgery on Mr. Kelso?"

"I didn't see him or speak to him until he came into the operating theatre," replied Anna. She was speaking more carefully now, and her eyes flickered from Doug to Jamieson and back. "So I had no way of telling. And while he was operating, his voice wasn't slurred, he seemed to know exactly what he was doing, so I didn't have any concerns about him."

"That must have been most reassuring for you," said Douglas, "considering some of your previous operating experiences with him."

His sarcasm must have struck home, because two spots of red appeared on Anna's pale cheeks.

"Yes it was," she retorted. "It's hard enough doing my own job without having to worry about somebody else's."

"If you thought that the surgeon was incapable, for whatever reason, drugs, alcohol, what would you do?"

"I'd tell the surgeon to get someone else or cancel the case, then if he didn't, I'd call the hospital administrator and let him deal with it."

"Have you ever had occasion to do that with Mr. Kirkwall?"

Anna hesitated for the barest moment. "No," she said, "I have not."

To Jamieson's astonishment, Doug rather abruptly put his pen down and said, "That'll be all for now, Dr. McKenzie, thank you very kindly. If you think of anything else that might be of assistance, please let us know." He stood up, pulled an embossed business card with the crest of the Tayside Police from his wallet, and gave it to her. "I can be reached at that number at any time," he said.

"Why did you end the interview like that?" Jamieson asked after she had gone.

"Because I had all the information that we would get out of her," replied Douglas in a rather self-satisfied tone. "The main things we found out were that she likes Mr. Kirkwall, feels protective toward him, and last night probably wasn't the first time she got him out of trouble in the operating theatre. Secondly, she has no idea why Kelso died."

"I think she more than *likes* him," said Jamieson.

The phone rang. Doug expected the call to be for the absent supervisor, but the hospital operators were already rerouting calls to him. It was Dr. Malcolm Anderson, the police surgeon, who was also the hospital's senior pathologist, and he sounded annoyed. "What's this about an autopsy on a hospital death?" he asked. "If we did a postmortem on everybody who happened to die in the hospital, we'd be backed up till next Christmas."

Doug explained the circumstances. "By the way," he asked Anderson, "do you know who the patient was?"

"How the hell should I know? I just heard about the case a few minutes ago."

"It was Robertson Kelso."

There was an astonished silence, followed by a long exhalation. "It'll be my pleasure," said Dr. Anderson in a quite different voice. "We can dissect the bastard tomorrow morning at ten."

Chapter 7

Fiona opened the door for Hugh Kirkwall. He was usually fairly casual about his appearance, but now he looked positively disheveled, his tie loose, and too-long dark hair all over the place. He was good-looking in a harassed kind of way, thought Fiona, glancing at the distraught brown eyes and the deep lines in his face. He looked as if he might have lost some weight, judging by the way his clothes hung on him.

"Please come in, Mr. Kirkwall," she said, smiling.

"Oh, yes, thanks," he said, glancing at his watch, then looked uncomfortably past Fiona into the house. "You must be Jean's daughter.... I hate to bother you all at home like this...."

"Not at all," replied Fiona, who had inherited her mother's hospitality gene. She stood to one side of the door so he could pass. "Mum's made a great dinner."

Mr. Kirkwall smiled at Fiona, a shy, insecure smile, and suddenly she felt that she liked this man. He appealed to her motherly feelings, and

she wanted to straighten his tie and take a vigor-
ous comb to his hair.

Steven was sitting in the living room reading
the *Courier* when Fiona showed him in. The television was on, and the evening news was about to
start. Steven put the paper down, stood up, shook
hands with Mr. Kirkwall and offered him a drink.

Kirkwall shook his head. "Just tonic, thanks,"
he said. "I've had my last and final alcoholic
drink yesterday."

Steven nodded, not knowing quite what to say,
and went over to the sideboard, where the drinks
were kept. "Ice?" he asked, the yellow-labeled
bottle of tonic water in his hand.

"No thanks." Kirkwall was so obviously tense
that Steven felt the need of a second sherry for
himself, which he poured and quickly gulped
down with his back turned to the visitor; it would
have been inconsiderate to drink in front of a man
so recently on the wagon.

Dinner was not a particularly joyful occasion.
Mrs. Findlay, Jean's mother, who was living with
them after breaking her hip some months before,
was startled to see an unfamiliar face at the dinner
table and stared questioningly at him throughout
the meal, although, of course, Jean had introduced
Hugh and had explained that Mr. Kirkwall was
one of her hospital colleagues.

After dinner, Mrs. Findlay went back up to her
room, and Steven went upstairs to finish reading
the paper in their bedroom. The girls tidied up

and did the dishes while Hugh followed Jean into the living room.

During the meal, Hugh had managed to make some small talk, but now his tension was painfully evident again. A thin rim of sweat had formed just below his hairline, and Jean wondered if he was having withdrawal symptoms in addition to his other anxieties.

They sat down.

"How can I help you, Hugh?" asked Jean in her most sympathetic tone. She sat facing him, her hands in her lap.

"I don't know," said Hugh, in an agony of discomfort. "I suppose it was silly of me to even think about it, but I thought you might know how to . . ." He paused, unsure how to go on. "You see, Jean, I think I've been set up, in some kind of a way." He told her about Shah's bringing in the police, how unrelenting his antagonism had been. Hugh's voice shook, and he almost broke down when he told Jean that he felt a hairsbreadth from having his hospital and operating privileges withdrawn, and that would happen, he felt sure, as soon as Sandy Michie eventually gave in to Shah's unremitting pressure.

"Why is Dr. Shah like that, do you think, Hugh?" asked Jean. "Everybody knows that he's jealous and wants to replace you in the hospital hierarchy, but . . . is there some other reason why he'd try to get you in trouble?"

"Yes, there is." Hugh knew exactly why and when Shah had turned seriously against him. To

Hugh, it hadn't been a big deal, but to Shah, it most certainly had. About a year before, around the time Frances and Hugh were having the worst of their problems, and Hugh was getting increasingly upset about the situation, Sandy Michie's nine-year-old son Alex had developed severe abdominal pain and was brought to the emergency room by his mother, Kate. Dr. Shah had been on duty at the time, and examined the boy. He'd reported to Kate that Alex had acute inflammation of the bowel, and would probably need an urgent operation. Kate had panicked and called her husband Sandy out of a meeting. Both Sandy and Kate insisted that they wanted Hugh Kirkwall to see Alex, and Shah phoned him. Unfortunately, it turned out to be at a most inconvenient time, when Frances and Hugh were in the middle of a tense discussion.

"No, this case absolutely cannot wait, Mr. Kirkwall," Shah had told Hugh in his persistent, singsong voice. "The child is acutely ill and in my opinion will need to be operated upon immediately."

Frances, close to tears, fastened on the incident. "Hugh, you're just too busy for our marriage to work. I never get to spend any time with you, and all your energy goes into your work."

Heartsick, Hugh picked his car keys off the hook in the kitchen. "I'm sorry, Frances," he said. "We can talk about it when I come back, but I have to go in. It's an emergency. . . ."

As he backed out of the garage, Frances came

out of the front door and watched as he drove down the road toward the hospital.

When Hugh got to the emergency room, examined Alex, and found that he was suffering from nothing worse than constipation, he lost his temper with Dr. Shah, loudly enough so that others heard him. Alex was given a gentle enema, and went home cured. His parents were too relieved to be upset with Dr. Shah, but Shah felt that he had been totally humiliated, and never forgave Hugh. When Hugh got home that day, Frances was gone. After Hugh had started drinking heavily, Shah had begun to exact his revenge. His hatred of Hugh, who was popular with most of the staff, became a topic of uneasy conversation around the hospital.

Hugh explained all this to Jean. "If Shah had been anyone else," he went on, "I'd have taken him out for a drink and a talk, and we'd have straightened out our differences, because in a hospital, everybody has to be able to work with everyone else. But you can't do that with Shah. He's too self-righteous, and anyway he had no desire to end the quarrel. He's just not a person one can speak frankly and honestly with."

"But what about Robertson Kelso, Hugh?" Jean sounded uncomfortable. "What with Frances and everything . . . Wouldn't it have been wiser to have asked another surgeon to operate on him?"

"There wasn't anybody else. Frank Grant's away, and Eric Lumsden is sick with the flu. And

Kelso was far too ill to transport to Dundee. No, I had to do it, although, of course, operating on that man was the last thing I wanted to do."

"Did anything happen during the operation that might have led to his death?"

"No, not really. There was a problem with bleeding, but we fixed it. He had a drop in pressure, but it wasn't bad, and it didn't last long. It was back to normal by the time we finished." Hugh passed a hand over his forehead. "Of course, the suture might have slipped off the artery again, and he could have bled out during his sleep, but ..." Hugh shook his head. "I'm just about certain that that didn't happen."

"Well, it sounds as if there's going to be a formal inquiry, so they'll do an autopsy, won't they? And if they don't find an obvious cause of death, that'll clear you, surely?"

"Maybe. But you know how people are. Everybody will think that somehow I was responsible, and some will even say I killed him because of Frances. If they do find an obvious cause of death, and it was my fault, I'll certainly take the responsibility. But if there isn't ... well, you know how gossip starts. In no time they'll start talking about poisons, stuff like that."

Jean looked at him with astonishment. "Poisons? Why would anyone even suggest that?"

"Oh, I don't know." Hugh's restlessness seemed to be getting worse. He stood up and paced around the room. "In a town like this, a reputation is easily destroyed, and that's what Shah is trying to do to me."

"Hugh, what can I do to help?" Jean's voice was sympathetic, and her offer of help was sincere, but she also felt that a good part of Hugh's problems had been brought about by himself.

Hugh came back to his chair and sat down, then moved his body restlessly forward until he was balanced on the precarious edge of it. "I don't know, Jean. I suppose I just needed to talk to someone about it, someone who knows the scene and the people." He looked thoughtfully at Jean, as if he had been so immersed in his problems that he was seeing her for the first time, and smiled diffidently. "And, of course, you do have a reputation for finding the answer to ... difficult problems."

"Well," Jean answered, "you know that you can always come here and talk. We've known each other for a long time."

She could see that Hugh's tension was diminishing, perhaps because of the calm surroundings here in the Montrose household. It didn't occur to her that it was her own composure and common-sense attitude that had calmed him, and also that she'd allowed him to say what was on his mind and come to his own conclusions.

"Well, I'll just have to wait until after the autopsy," he said, standing up and squaring his shoulders. "But if it doesn't show a clear cause of death, and I feel pretty sure that it won't, I'll have to find out if somebody did kill him."

He paused, and a shadow of his old crinkly smile crossed his face. "But I wouldn't know how to do that, so I suppose that's really why I came to see you."

Chapter 8

Earlier that day, after Doug finished talking to Anna McKenzie, he found that the other hospital employees who had been involved with Robertson Kelso the evening before were not available now. Doris Caie, the emergency room nurse, was off until three that afternoon, as was Rosemary Gallacher, the night supervisor. Rosemary had done a double shift that night and had not left the hospital until seven in the morning. As there was no evidence yet that any crime had been committed, Doug didn't feel entitled to disturb their well-earned rest.

Dr. Shah was hanging around when they left the office, obviously anxious to talk to Douglas, but Doug felt no immediate need for further conversation with him, so he merely nodded briskly to Shah and marched past, accompanied by Jamieson.

Shah watched them, his face expressionless, but he was gripped by an overwhelming anxiety. He knew about their antipathy; he was used to that. The dour Scots, and in particular the people of

Perth, were so clannish, so insular, that no one with a darker skin or a different way of speaking could ever hope to be accepted into their inner circle. Look at the way they'd treated him at the Dundee clinic—if the same problem had happened to one of their own people, they would have overlooked it, but because he was a foreigner, they had got rid of him. Shah didn't even really care about that, because he despised them, all of them. He didn't like to socialize, unless it was in order to push himself forward professionally.

He didn't allow Madhur, his wife, to join any clubs or mix with anyone. They never entertained, and as far as he was concerned, his wife was there to take care of his needs, and that was it. Back in Bombay, where they had both been brought up, the women liked to get together during the day, and laugh and chatter and giggle. He had intensely disapproved of that. Here in Perth, he didn't have to worry. For one thing, the local women didn't seem to have that kind of herd instinct; and then they didn't like Madhur. Maybe it was because Madhur's unsmiling face was pockmarked and sallow, or maybe because she didn't have much of a grasp of the English language. He shrugged. When he thought about Madhur, the concept of love never even crossed Shah's mind. It never had. He'd married her because their parents had agreed that they were a suitable match, and she'd brought some money with her, enough for them to leave the overcrowded Bombay medi-

cal scene and go to Britain. Madhur rarely spoke
to him, she never smiled or changed her expression, but as long as his clothes were clean and
carefully ironed, and his food was on time, he
didn't care about that, either. Madhur had little
education, read with difficulty, so they had little
in common. Most of the time he simply ignored
her existence.

Shah looked at his watch. It was fifteen minutes
before the start of the hospital's Quality Assurance
Committee meeting, and his anxiety had to do
with what he would say there, and how he would
say it. As he well knew, he was on the QAC only
because most of his colleagues hated serving on
that particular committee, which had the task of
reviewing difficult cases, and occasionally having
to censure doctors for the way they had handled
them. Shah had quickly recognized the potential
power of the committee, and tried to turn it into
a weapon to intimidate other physicians. In doing
so, he had clashed on numerous occasions with
the chairman, Hugh Kirkwall. In the past, the
meetings lasted about forty minutes, but not since
the advent of Dr. Shah. He picked away at everything, wanted a full discussion of the most trivial
details, often missing the more important points,
and generally annoying everyone there.

The committee usually met in the first-floor hospital conference room, a fine, spacious oak-
paneled place with high, leather-backed chairs
around a long table. It had originally been built
for the exclusive use of the Hospital Board, but as

their meetings took place only once a month, Sandy Michie had decided to open it for more general use.

Most of the QAC members, including Sandy Michie, who represented the hospital management, were already seated when Shah walked in. It was obvious that they were discussing Robertson Kelso when he entered, because they all stopped speaking, and Hugh Kirkwall watched him with a cold stare as he came into the room and sat down.

Today, to everyone's relief and surprise, Shah was very restrained during most of the meeting, and actually said very little until after the last case had been discussed and corrective action suggested. Hugh was about to bring the meeting to a close when Shah stood up.

"Mr. Kirkwall, gentlemen," he said in his formal way. "I am sure you all know about the unfortunate events surrounding the admission of Mr. Robertson Kelso to the hospital yesterday evening, and his subsequent death early this morning. As the case will no doubt be referred to this committee for action, and as Mr. Kirkwall is intimately concerned with the case, and because of the serious allegations that have been made concerning his role in the patient's death, I would respectfully suggest that Mr. Kirkwall take this opportunity to resign his chairmanship of this committee, as of today."

There was a shocked silence. The other members glanced uneasily at each other.

Hugh, his face suddenly flushed, said quietly, "If the members of this committee feel the same way, I'd be happy to . . ."

Sandy Michie stood up abruptly and interrupted, his voice tight with suppressed anger, and addressed Shah. "Your suggestion is totally inappropriate, Dr. Shah," he said. "The case of Robertson Kelso is at present under investigation, and at this time there is no indication whatsoever that Mr. Kirkwall or anyone else was at fault. Secondly," he went on, his eyes fixed angrily on Shah, "chairmen of hospital committees are appointed by the Supervisory Board, and only the board has the power to institute such changes."

"Of course," replied Shah, not at all taken aback, "I am aware of that. I am simply wishing to avoid the problems that will no doubt arise when the matter becomes public. The fact that the person principally involved in the case is also the chairman of the committee, whose job it is to investigate such events, will also come to their attention, and that will lead not only to a further loss of public confidence in this hospital, but possibly to a major investigation by the Tayside Health Board—and also by the police."

"The police are already involved, thanks to you," replied Michie curtly. "And now, if that's all right with Mr. Kirkwall, I suggest that we adjourn this meeting."

Usually, the committee members would hang around for a little while to chat, but not this time. They all had urgent business elsewhere, it seemed, and Hugh noticed that most of them didn't look him in the eye when they left.

Dr. Shah, however, was well pleased. He could see the writing on the wall as well as anyone, and the chairmanship of the hospital's Quality Assurance Committee finally seemed to be coming within his grasp.

That morning, when the rooks in the big ash tree opposite were just beginning their cawing din, Doris Caie was lying awake in her bed, a prey to all kinds of fears. Now she realized that it hadn't been very clever of her to phone Albert the evening before, and tell him that Robertson Kelso had been admitted, but how could she *not* have told him? His reaction had alarmed her, but not as much as his sudden appearance did, just before eleven, in the emergency room, when the staff was changing and she was about to go off duty. To someone who didn't know Albert, he would have looked perfectly normal, but she knew and recognized the signs: the tightness of the mouth, the quickness of his movements, and the cold bright look in his eye when he came up to the desk.

"Where is he?" he asked quietly.

"You shouldn't have come here," she replied, almost in a whisper. "I'm just about to start report."

He gripped the edge of the desk. "Where is he?" His voice was calm, but there was a kind of emphasis in his repetition that scared her. Doris wasn't normally afraid of Albert, even in one of his moods, but now she was. She could sense the tension, the pent-up violence in his voice, in his whole body language.

"He's had his operation," she told him. Out of the corner of her eye, she could see Kevin Souttar waiting to get report from her, watching through the sliding-glass office window. "He'll be back in his room by now, I suppose."

"What's the room number?"

Doris was getting really afraid now, but she didn't dare do anything except give him his answers. She pressed a few keys, then checked the computer screen. "He was admitted to room 412," she said, "so I suppose that's where he is. It's up on the fourth floor, where they put the private patients." She looked at him with a growing panic. "Albert, you can't go up there. . . ."

But Albert was already walking down the corridor away from her, with that awful limp that he had now, but moving fast enough to make the tails of his old brown raincoat trail behind him.

He hadn't come home until almost two o'clock. When he did come in, he was breathing hard. He clumped up the stairs to the bedroom, his limp even more pronounced, then flung his clothes off and came painfully into the bed. He wouldn't speak to her, or answer her questions. They both lay awake, silent, hearing each other breathe, but separated, she knew, by their joint obsession with Robertson Kelso.

Albert was trained as an accountant, and inherited the practice that his father, Arthur, started

when he came back from the war in 1945. Arthur
had been a careful, canny man, and over the years,
earned an unshakable reputation for integrity and
honesty, if not for imagination. As thrifty as one
would expect an accountant to be, Arthur had
married late, and was forty-four years old when
Albert was born. The business, which occupied
the second floor of a building on Charlotte Street,
near the west end of the old bridge, had remained
small and exclusive, by Arthur's choice. He dealt
with old-established firms, a few wealthy individuals and trusts, and after several years, had gradually built up a practice that made up for its lack
of size by the respect it had earned in the business
community of Perth. When Arthur decided to re-
tire, Albert, who had done his accounting training
at Glasgow University, took over. He was full of
energy and new ideas, and within a few weeks,
there was a new carpet in the office, the old
wooden filing cabinets had been replaced by a fine
new computerized system, and Arthur's three
middle-aged clerks were gone; their places taken
by two young, computer-trained women he'd
brought in from Glasgow. Within six months Albert had turned the quiet practice upside down,
terminated a number of old accounts that weren't
bringing in enough money, and was actively looking for additional business.

And that was when he met Robertson Kelso, an
up-and-coming entrepreneur who had inherited a
prospering business and who was actively starting
new ones in the area, to the point where he was

becoming one of the more important figures in town. Kelso was also known to have engaged in some sharp business practices, and had acquired a dubious reputation among the generally staid and conservative Perth businessmen.

When Albert told his father that he was considering taking Kelso on as a client, old Arthur was horrified, but Albert was certain that his future lay in acquiring this type of wealthy, entrepreneurial client, and paid no attention to him.

Albert and Kelso met in the Theatre Restaurant, and within minutes Albert was caught in the spell, as others had been before him, of Robertson Kelso's swashbuckling presence, matched as it seemed by a progressive and visionary way of doing business. He was the most exciting man Albert had ever met, full of ideas and plans to take over the world, starting modestly with the city of Perth.

"It's all about fish," he told Albert, pointing at him with his fork over a fine Dover sole. "It's a diminishing resource worldwide, and prices are going sky-high."

"We've already got a whole lot of fish farms here," Albert diffidently pointed out. "A couple of them closed this year already. Apparently, the fish give each other funguses or diseases that can't be cured, and die."

Kelso shrugged his shoulders. "Ach, these folks are just amateurs," he said contemptuously. "And worse than that, they don't have any imagination. They just enclose a pond or a stretch of water, feed the fish, and hope that Mother Nature will do the rest. That's what they used to do with chickens until somebody figured out how to grow them in batteries, and that's when the chicken industry took off. Now, when our smelts reach a certain size, we put them in individual pens with filtered, oxygenated water flowing at a predetermined speed, and feed them scientifically planned diets. It takes half as long for them to grow to full weight, it costs less, they don't infect each other, and the quality's superb. . . ."

Kelso asked Albert a lot of questions about how he had reorganized his father's accounting practice.

"But if it's all on the computer," he asked, "what if there's a power failure, or your hard drive crashes?"

"We back everything up," Albert replied, full of confidence in the system he'd purchased. "The last job of the day is to make floppy disk and tape copies of everything and keep them in a fireproof safe in my office. So even if the place burns down in the night, I still have all my records. It's a hundred percent foolproof."

By the time lunch was over, they had made a deal that would be reasonably lucrative for Albert. He would consolidate the accounts of Kelso's various businesses, do the audits, and prepare tax returns. It was by far the biggest account Caie & Caie had ever handled, and Albert went back to his office in great high spirits.

For a while, all went well. Albert put in vast

amounts of time and energy on Kelso's businesses, but he was finding out things that made him very uneasy. Finally, he got his courage up, went to Kelso's office, and confronted him.

"I'm sorry, Mr. Kelso, but some of the things you're doing are illegal," he said, after outlining the problem. "Even with privately held companies like yours, you can't flout basic accounting principles. You've been hiding taxable assets in companies that have no employees, no products, and have only a name and a post office box address." Albert took a deep breath. "I'm sorry, Mr. Kelso, but under the law I will be forced to report this to the tax authorities."

While Albert spoke, Kelso had been getting red in the face, but after he finished, Kelso put his big hands on the desk and nodded. "Of course, Albert. If you're prepared for the inevitable consequences of such an act, go ahead. Otherwise, you'd be well advised to just go on doing your job and shut up."

"What inevitable consequences?" Albert had heard people talk about certain of Kelso's business methods, but he didn't believe them. Nevertheless, there was something frightening about Kelso's expression as he stared at Albert across his desk.

"Look, Albert, let's be realistic," said Kelso, pushing his chair away from the desk. "I'm by far your biggest account. All I want you to do is go along with things the way they are. That way we'll both do very nicely. The only reason you know what you know is because I've given you that information, and there's no way the tax people on their own could figure it out. Which makes you an accessory before, during, and after the fact—I'm sure you understand that." Without waiting for a reply, he went on, in a voice that chilled Albert. "You asked about the consequences. I'm a bad man to cross, Albert, you should know that by now. Ask your friends. And aside from just ruining you . . ."

Listening openmouthed, Albert couldn't believe that this was the same man he'd bantered and joked with over the past several months. Kelso leaned forward, and his eyes took on a gleam that Albert didn't recognize. ". . . I can make you wish you'd never been born."

Albert stood up precipitately, almost knocking his chair over in the process. "You can't threaten me like this, Mr. Kelso. I've got my professional reputation to consider, and I certainly don't want to go to jail with you when the tax people find out what you're up to. I'm sorry, but I'll have to do what I have to do."

That same night, Albert's office was broken into, the computer was destroyed, and the safe was cracked and the contents stolen. A week later, after Albert had closed the office and gone around the back to where his car was parked, three men appeared as he was opening the car door. One of them hit him over the head with a short club, then they smashed his legs with an iron bar. It was all over in a minute; they pushed him into his car, closed the door, and were gone. Nobody ever found them, or discovered who they had been.

When Albert came back to the office after two weeks in the hospital, there was practically no business to come back to; with his wheelchair, he couldn't even get up the steps without help. During his absence, his two assistants had been repeatedly threatened by telephone, and both had decided to return to Glasgow. Most of his remaining businesses and trusts decided to find an accounting firm where at least someone was there to answer the phone.

But the last straw was a series of lawsuits started by Kelso against Albert, alleging everything from professional negligence to loss of documents and purveyance of improper financial advice, and Albert didn't have the money to defend himself. He finally closed down his business, and went out looking for a job with one of his old competitors; but at this point his local reputation was in tatters, and they were all too afraid of Robertson Kelso to employ him.

After that, the only thing that kept Albert Caie going was his blinding hatred of Robertson Kelso, a hatred that grew and festered as his personal fortunes declined. The worst thing was that there was nothing he could do, however he racked his brain to find a way to get revenge. He couldn't fight Kelso in the courts, and the records he had put together on Kelso's businesses had been stolen. He'd thought of marching up to him, either at home or at the office, and shooting him, and had even bought a gun with that in mind. Albert's fantasies of various forms of painful death for Robertson Kelso were the last thing he thought about at night, and the first thing that his mind locked on to in the morning.

Fortunately, for him, his wife Doris was a trained nurse and had gone back to work at the hospital, and only her modest income had saved them from bankruptcy and total disaster.

And now ... Doris woke when Albert stirred, and she lay in the bed, her eyes closed, with a deepening feeling of dread. Something terrible had happened during the night, she was certain of it, but she also knew that Albert wouldn't say a word to her about it. He'd always been a reticent man, but since the business with Robertson Kelso, he'd gone further and further into himself, into his own world of anger and bitterness and hatred. Doris loved him, of course. It was a quiet, undemanding kind of love, one that stayed out of the way when the demons were upon him, a love that was there for him when it was needed. Now the demons were in possession, howling around inside his head—she could almost hear them scratching and clawing at the membranes of his brain. They were there, in full and terrifying strength, and she stayed quiet, keeping her breathing rate slow and regular, so that he wouldn't know that she was awake.

Chapter 9

Jean decided to attend Robertson Kelso's postmortem for two reasons. One was that Kelso had been her patient, the other was that she'd promised Hugh Kirkwall that she would do what she could to find out what had really happened. And, of course, a certain amount of plain human curiosity had also entered into the decision.

She parked her car in the area nearest the pathology department. This wasn't her first visit there, and as she walked past the laundry, past the rows of silent gray canvas hampers with PRI stenciled on them in black letters, she thought of other victims she had seen in this place, Bobby Sutherland, Moira Dalgleish . . . She shivered at the thoughts and memories that passed through her mind.

Jean opened the door marked STAFF ONLY and walked in, past a few closed doors with frosted glass windows, to where the hallway expanded into a kind of small vestibule outside the double doors of the autopsy room. There were a few plastic chairs and a round Formica-topped table on one side of the doors and on the other side, an old off-white coffee machine stood incongruously on a metal table in the corner. Douglas Niven was there standing next to the table, talking quietly to Constable Jamieson.

A red light shone above the autopsy room door. "Dr. Anderson's in there," said Doug, indicating the doors when Jean came up. Jamieson stared into space, not acknowledging her presence. In turn, Jean ignored him. A tiny smile appeared on Doug's lips, and he went on, still addressing Jean. "He's doing some old woman whose dogs turned on her yesterday morning. Poor old thing, she didn't have enough money to feed them, so they finally took matters into their own hands, so to speak."

Jean shuddered. At that moment the red light went out, and the door hissed open. Dr. Malcolm Anderson came out, pulling off his mask. He was wearing a long, bloodstained rubber apron over his greens, and a pair of once-green shin-high rubber boots that Dracula would have seriously coveted.

"Ah, there you are." He looked at Jean and smiled. Dr. Anderson always had a soft spot for Jean. "Glad you could come, *quine*," he said, addressing her in his gruff Aberdeenshire dialect. *Quine*, Jean knew, meant *girl*, derived from the word *queen*, and that was how he always addressed her. He spoke as if he'd invited them all to a rather select dinner party.

"It's always a pleasure, Malcolm," murmured Jean.

"Is Mr. Kirkwall coming?" asked Dr. Anderson. "He usually comes to postmortems that he's been involved in."

"No he isn't," said Douglas firmly. "And that's because he *was* involved in this case."

Anderson nodded. "Brian's started on him," he said, jerking his head toward the autopsy room. His eyes lit up, like a boy about to show one of his special treasures. "By the way, would you like to see what's left of the widow Nelligan?"

"The lady with the dogs? No thanks, Malcolm." Jean shook her head decisively.

"Oh, all right." Dr. Anderson's face fell slightly. "It was just very interesting, how the bigger dogs went for the neck and torso, and the smaller ones for the arms and lower legs. You can tell by the size and shape of the teeth marks."

"Law of the jungle," said Jamieson unexpectedly, and they turned for a second to look at him. He blushed slightly and looked at the floor.

"You know the Humane Society people killed the dogs." Anderson went on as if Jamieson didn't exist. "But the most interesting part is that she was dead before they started to eat her. She had a massive stroke. The clot in her carotid artery was almost a foot long."

He looked at them with an expression of naive delight mixed with a little pride, as if he were waiting for a discreet burst of applause. It didn't come.

"Have you read Mr. Kelso's chart?" asked Doug.

"No. I was about to do that now." Dr. Anderson picked up the slim chart. It was in a beige folder, held together with four rubber bands. He flipped the bands off with practiced ease, opened the folder, and scanned the contents, then looked up and grinned at them. "The only thing that surprised me, knowing about Kelso, was that he wasn't brought in here with a knife sticking out of his back or his chest full of bullets."

"Maybe he was," said Douglas. "That's what we're here to find out. Maybe we untrained personnel just didn't see the weapons."

"We did a toxicology check," said Anderson. "On the blood samples they drew when he came in, and samples drawn this morning. There's nothing on the preliminaries except a trace of curare in this morning's sample, but we'll have a full report by this time tomorrow."

"Curare?" asked Douglas, his interest perking up. "Isn't that some kind of South American Indian arrow poison?"

"Yes it is," said Anderson, grinning at him. "But of course curarelike drugs are also used in anesthesia as muscle relaxants. The amounts found were consistent with the amount on record given during the operation."

Douglas glowered at Dr. Anderson and mumbled something inaudible. He should have thought of those muscle relaxants and Jamieson's almost imperceptible grin didn't help matters. "Anything else?" Doug asked brusquely. "Like, I don't know, arsenic, or something like that?"

"No, not so far. But they're doing the whole spectrum, everything from aspirin to Zyloprim. If he was poisoned, we'll know it tomorrow."

"I didn't realize that anybody had even suggested that he'd been poisoned." Jean remembered Hugh Kirkwall's comment.

"We're just checking out all the possibilities we can think of, Jean," said Douglas quietly. "And that's because Kelso was such a . . . notorious individual. There must be a lot of people rejoicing today."

"And also because that Dr. Shah chap has been making a fuss, as usual," added Dr. Anderson. "And, as usual, everybody's trying to cover their . . . exposed parts," he went on, glancing amusedly at Jean. "Which gives all of us additional and unnecessary work." He shrugged, and rubbed the side of his nose with a bloody glove. "Actually, it sounds as if Kelso most likely died of one of those postoperative cardiac arrhythmias that are very difficult to demonstrate at autopsy." He sighed, as if Kelso had deliberately planned it that way, just to add to Dr. Anderson's already heavy burden.

The speaker over the door clicked, then the quiet voice of Brian Thomson, the mortuary attendant, came over the intercom. "He's ready, Dr. Anderson," he said.

Jean took a deep breath, feeling that this would be the last lungful of unpolluted air she'd be taking in for a while, and followed the others through the double doors. Actually, the smell inside was less pungent than the last time she'd been there; but, of course, that had been at the autopsy of Moira Dalgleish's long-drowned body. Remembering the eel, Jean shivered momentarily, then squared her shoulders, unable to prevent herself from glancing at the only other occupied table, where, presumably, lay the uneaten remains of the widow Nelligan. Fortunately, the table was now covered by a white sheet.

Robertson Kelso managed to be imposing even when lying dead on the slab. His naked body was large and muscular, and even the pallor in his stiffened face didn't seem to remove the malignant aura around him. His IV tubes had been cut off in the approved manner, leaving the cannulas still in position, anchored to the skin with adhesive tape, just as Anna McKenzie had placed them.

Dr. Anderson pulled the ceiling-mounted, sound-activated microphone toward him. "The body is that of Robertson Kelso," he intoned in the particularly flat tone that pathologists everywhere use when dictating autopsy findings. "He has been identified to me by Dr. Jean Montrose, his family physician . . ." He raised his eyebrows at Jean, who nodded. "A recent incision is noted in the right lower quadrant of the abdomen," he went on, "consistent with the reported appendectomy performed"—he looked up at the clock—"approximately thirty-four hours ago."

With Brian's help, he turned the body first to one side, then to the other. "There is no sign of entry or exit wounds on the body . . ." Dr. Anderson winked over his mask at Doug, then looked back at the side of the body. "Livedo reticularis is less than would be expected . . ."

"What's that?" whispered Jamieson to Doug. "Libido something?"

"Livedo reticularis," said Douglas in a superior tone. "It means that purple color in the back and dependent parts of the body. It's when blood drains down after death, under the influence of gravity."

Jamieson was going to pursue the topic, but he saw Dr. Anderson staring sternly at him. Dr. Anderson did not permit private conversations while an autopsy was in progress.

With Brian Thomson's assistance, Dr. Anderson then opened the chest and abdomen. The noise of the electric saw cutting through the breast bone set Jean's teeth on edge, and she stood back to avoid the shower of sawdustlike bone fragments that shot out from under the vibrating blade.

As soon as the chest and abdominal cavities were open, Dr. Anderson picked up a long, porcelain-handled knife and deftly cut across the lower neck structures, then, with a flourish pulled the heart and lungs out of the chest like a conjurer pulling a rabbit out of a bag. The dislocated organs made a slurping noise that made Jamieson go approximately the same color as Robertson Kelso. He stepped back and leaned against the wall, sweat on his forehead.

"Would you like a glass of water?" Jean asked him, not without a touch of malice. He said nothing, but shook his head emphatically. Ever since Jean had accidentally almost killed him in a deserted house some years before, Jamieson had harbored an irrational but implacable resentment against her.

Holding the entrails like a butcher holds a plucked chicken, Dr. Anderson took the heart and lungs to a wooden cutting board next to the table, and after examining the coronary arteries, sliced open the heart, looking at each of the four cavities. He didn't say anything, but a frown formed and deepened on his brow, and he seemed puzzled by something.

Then they examined the operation site. All the tissues were matted together, but Anderson pushed his gloved fingers between the tissue planes, and quickly separated them. The appendix stump was securely closed. "And this is all right, too," he said, pointing with a long forceps at a knot of black thread. "The appendiceal artery is tied, and there certainly wasn't any bleeding from that source."

He pushed the loops of gray bowel aside and carefully examined the back of the abdominal cavity. There was a small amount of pinkish blood-stained fluid, essentially a normal finding. "Look at the blood vessels," he said to Jean in a strange voice. "They're practically empty. Here. Look at the inferior vena cava." He indicated a flattened gray tube running down the right side of the back of the abdominal wall, about an inch wide, the biggest vein in the body. "Normally, it's full of blood . . ." He took a pair of big scissors attached to the table by a long metal chain, and cut through the big vein. Only a trickle of dark, almost black blood came out.

"That is really very strange," he said, but it was the tone of Dr. Anderson's voice more than his words that made the hairs on the back of Jean's neck stand up on end. Against all her experience and training, she felt as if she were in the presence of something frightening, something she couldn't see but that she could feel, something silent and unutterably evil emanating from Robertson Kelso's open body.

"Let's see . . ." went on Dr. Anderson, still in that odd, subdued voice. He picked up the chart, flipped through the pages until he came to the anesthesia record. "Here we are. He was given over a liter of Ringer's lactate . . . received no transfused blood . . ." He turned a page. "The anesthetist estimated blood loss at about 750 milliliters, which is about a pint and a half. . . ." He stared at the chart, then at Jean, and in a disbelieving tone said, "There's hardly any blood in this body. Quite frankly, *quine,* I don't understand this at all. Apparently, he didn't bleed very much during the operation, and we've established that there wasn't any internal hemorrhage . . . He wasn't shot or stabbed. . . ."

Dr. Anderson tried to grin, but it was obvious that he was seriously shaken. "There aren't any vampires loose up at the hospital, are there?"

Chapter 10

After leaving the pathology department, Jean went back to her surgery, feeling unaccountably frightened and pensive. It was hard for her to even consider that any unnatural phenomena had been involved in Robertson Kelso's death, but there didn't seem to be any rational explanation for the autopsy findings. She was glad she'd found the courage to go, because otherwise it would have been difficult to visualize a body in whom most of the blood seemed to have disappeared. Could it have been reabsorbed out of the blood vessels into the tissues? She'd asked that question of Dr. Anderson. He'd never heard of such a thing happening; but he too was puzzled and confused, so he was willing to entertain any kind of sensible explanation. "We'll see for sure when we examine the tissues under the microscope," he had said, shaking his head. "If the red cells have somehow migrated outside the blood vessels, we'll see them," he went on. He smiled rather unsurely at her. "Then we'll write a paper that'll revolutionize the entire science and study of pathology."

But as she drove down the hill from the hospital, at the back of Jean's mind lurked all the tales she'd been hearing about for weeks and scoffed at, all those stories of unnatural happenings in the Perth area. Both Lisbie and Fiona had been bringing daily accounts of these unlikely stories home. Malcolm Anderson had mentioned vampires, but of course he was just joking, and Jean firmly put the idea out of her head.

She didn't have long to ruminate on the fate of Robertson Kelso. She parked in the street outside the surgery, and walked up the short flagstoned path, stepping around the puddles left by an early-morning shower. Eleanor, her secretary, looked relieved to see her. "Mrs. Kelso's here with Jeff," she said. "He's very upset about his father."

"Oh, dear," said Jean, thinking that Jeff must be the only person in all the world who wasn't happy that Robertson Kelso was dead.

Jeff was a slender, pale-faced eleven-year-old boy with the same expression and coloring as his mother; and like his mother, he didn't smile or look Jean in the eye when she came in. There was a slight and probably permanent thickening of the tissues over his right eye, from what had been reported as a fall down the stairs some weeks previously.

With a spontaneous gesture of affection, Jean put her arms around both of them and gave them a hug. "Come in to my office," she said. "Would you like a cup of tea?" she asked Irene, who shook her head. "How about you, Jeff? Would you like something? We have some chocolate Penguins."

Jeff, red-eyed, shook his head wordlessly.

"Say 'No thank you, Dr. Montrose,' Jeff," chided Irene gently.

"That's all right," said Jean, leading the way into her office. She closed the door behind them. "Are you remembering to take your insulin regularly?" she asked Irene, concerned that the death of her husband might have made her ignore her medical needs.

Irene started, and glanced quickly at Jean. A faint blush came over her damaged face. "I'm all right," she said. "It's Jeff I'm concerned about. He isn't sleeping, and he cries most of the time. He says . . . Jeff, tell Dr. Montrose what you told me."

Jeff looked at the floor and said nothing.

"Do you want me to tell Dr. Montrose, or will you tell her?"

Jeff didn't move.

"He says that . . ." Irene Kelso put a hand on Jeff's slim shoulders, as if she knew that she was betraying him. "He says that he did it. He keeps on saying it. That he killed his father."

Jean's mouth opened soundlessly.

Irene went on, speaking faster. "He says that he thought so much about killing him, and hoping that he would die, that it finally happened. He's sure that his thoughts were strong enough to kill him."

Jeff's eyes came up and looked at Jean with a

helpless, pained stillness that went straight to her heart. She knew that she would have to be very careful about what she said to him. Jeff was in a very fragile state of mind, and the wrong words might do permanent damage.

Jean took a deep breath. "Wishing somebody dead doesn't kill them, Jeff," she said quietly. "Everybody gets occasionally angry enough at someone to wish they were dead." She smiled at him. "So if the thoughts were enough to kill them, there wouldn't be too many people walking around today," she went on. "Just about everybody would be dead and buried."

"He did bad things to my mum," said Jeff, his voice barely audible. "That's why I wanted him to be dead. It wasn't because of what he did to me."

"He won't be doing any more bad things to either of you, Jeff. That part of your life and your mum's life is over, thank goodness. Now you can start all over again, lead a normal life, like the other children you know."

Jeff fixed Jean with an enormous intensity. "Are you *sure* you can't kill somebody like that? By thinking bad things about them?"

"I'm certain, Jeff. Absolutely certain."

Jeff moved a little toward his mother and took her hand.

"You're the man of the house now, Geoffrey Kelso," said Jean kindly. "And you're going to have to help take care of your mother."

"You mean make sure she takes her insulin?"

"Yes, things like that." Jean smiled at both of them.

"Jeff hasn't been sleeping," said Irene. "Should I give him a sleeping pill?"

"I'll tell you what I used to do when Lisbie was Jeff's age and couldn't sleep. I'd give her a little warm milk to drink, read her a story, one that would take her to faraway and wonderful places, like Baghdad or Tahiti. Usually, by the time I'd finished it, she'd be asleep."

"And if she wasn't?" Irene glanced doubtfully at Jeff.

"I'd start on another story. She never heard how the second one finished."

"Why the warm milk?" asked Irene, putting a protective arm around Jeff.

Jean smiled. "Psychology," she replied. "Lisbie soon associated the bedtime story with a sound sleep, and the warm milk reinforced the association."

Jean watched them leave, and felt a strange discomfort rising within her. Irene was so fiercely protective of Jeff, but it wasn't that that concerned her, or only indirectly. Irene might have been the last person to see Robertson Kelso alive, and she certainly had more than enough reason to want him dead, even if it was only for the protection of her son. And of course Irene had access to insulin, which as she surely knew, could kill, and was hard to trace unless special tests were carried out. It would have been an easy matter to inject the drug—she had been alone with him, and Kelso, still groggy from the operation, probably wouldn't even have noticed one more tiny needle being stuck in his arm. Also the needle hole would be too small to be visible at the autopsy, even if the pathologist were looking for it.

Hoping that she was wrong, Jean went back into her office and closed the door again.

Dr. Anderson was still in the department when she called.

"I don't suppose they did a postmortem blood sugar test on Kelso, did they, Malcolm?" she asked, her voice sounding very tentative, even to her. "Or an insulin assay on the tissues?"

"I don't think so. . . ." Anderson's voice suddenly changed. "My God, Jean, you're not telling me now that he was a diabetic?"

"No, he wasn't, as far as I know." There was a pause. "But his wife is."

"Oh, my God. Wait a minute." Jean could hear him put down the phone, and heard the rustle of papers on his desk. He was back on the line in a moment. "Okay, I'm looking at his chart. Let's see . . . His electrolytes on admission were normal . . . Here it is. Blood sugar, eighty milligrams percent. That's normal, and it's the only value we have."

"Is it too late to get a blood sugar now? And an insulin assay?"

Dr. Anderson sounded doubtful. "The blood sugar wouldn't tell us much at this stage, I wouldn't think, but we could certainly do an insulin assay. Good idea, *quine*. I'll see to it."

"Thanks, Malcolm. I hope I'm not wasting your time. It's probably a wild-goose chase, but who knows for sure?"

"With Robertson Kelso," said Dr. Anderson heavily, "I wouldn't be surprised by anything."

Chapter 11

Jean was already in the driveway and getting out of her car when she remembered that May Gallacher was coming to dinner. Luckily there was a whole roast chicken from Marks and Spencers in the refrigerator, and she decided to make that the basis of the meal. Before starting in the kitchen, she went upstairs to check on her mother, but Mrs. Findlay was fast asleep on the bed, fully dressed, a book still clutched in her hand. Very gently, so as not to wake her, Jean pulled the bedspread over her and went downstairs again.

She thought for a moment, then went to the oven and set it to preheat at 350 degrees. The chicken didn't take long; she pulled it into pieces, chopped the bigger chunks of meat into smaller chunks, using a big, black-handled knife from the set Steven had given her last Christmas, put the chicken pieces into the bottom of a big Pyrex dish, cut up a punnet of mushrooms and a bunch of asparagus, and threw the pieces in on top of the chicken, before submerging the whole thing in two tinfuls of condensed mushroom soup. Jean added a sprinkling of grated cheddar to the top, put on the glass lid, and popped the dish in the oven. Jean looked at the clock. The meal would be ready in exactly forty-five minutes, she knew from long experience; it wasn't exactly the first time she'd made this dish. Now all she had to do was make a big pot of spaghetti, which could wait for half an hour, so she went down to the basement and spent a few minutes tidying up the girls' rooms. They had both made their beds, sort of, but both of them had small items of clothing lying around, and Jean picked them up and took them upstairs to the laundry hamper. She thought briefly about taking a ten-minute rest before everybody came home, but if she fell asleep she'd have to wake up again, and then she'd feel grumpy and out of sorts for the rest of the day. All the time, at the back of her mind, lurked the image of Robertson Kelso, and she shivered, thinking of his weird, bloodless corpse lying on the autopsy table. With him in mind, she went up to the bathroom and washed her hands thoroughly, although she'd already washed them before starting to prepare dinner. A few minutes later she was back in the kitchen, pushing the stiff ends of a bunch of spaghetti into the boiling water and trying not to scald herself, when she heard the front door open and Lisbie and May came in.

Jean stopped to give them both a hug, then Lisbie took May by the hand and took her down to her room to show her some bead necklaces and bracelets that she'd made the previous weekend.

A few minutes later, after she'd salted the boiling spaghetti and was looking for the olive oil, Jean heard the front door open and close again, and looked at the clock with some satisfaction. When Steven came home from his job at the Perth Glassworks, he liked to have time for a quick look at the *Courier* then a glass of sherry with her before dinner.

He came in to the tiny kitchen and gave Jean a hug. "That smells wonderful," he said, wrinkling his nose appreciatively at the aroma coming from the oven. "What is it?"

Jean told him. "Would you reach the olive oil down for me, please?" she asked, pointing at the top shelf. "Fiona always puts it up there where I can't get at it."

"Sure, Shorty," replied Steven, smiling at her, and she punched him gently as he stretched up for the bottle.

"Just remember, dear," she said, "being short puts your vital organs nicely within my reach."

He laughed, handed her the bottle of olive oil, and kissed her lightly on the cheek. "You're sounding a wee bit aggressive today," he remarked. "Was everything all right down at the surgery?"

"They did Robertson Kelso's autopsy this morning," said Jean, suddenly somber. "And that sort of spoiled the rest of the day."

"You could have sold tickets for that event," said Steven, standing back as Jean poured a spoonful of oil over the bubbling spaghetti. "What did they find? A stake embedded in his heart, or something like that?"

Jean started, and stared at Steven. "No. But it's slightly weird that you should say that."

"Why?"

"Steven, dinner's going to be ready in a minute. We just have time for a quick sherry, if you like."

"Okay . . ." Steven looked curiously at her. Jean usually liked to tell him about the day's happenings, and the fact that she had cut him off suggested that something was seriously troubling her.

"I'm not trying to put you off, dear," she said, understanding his look. "I'm just not ready to talk about it yet. There was something so horrible about it . . ." Again Jean shuddered.

She followed Steven into the living room, and he went over to the sideboard and picked up the sherry bottle. He paused for a second, and then held the dark bottle up to the window. It was about a third full. "I just opened this yesterday, didn't I, Jean?" he asked, still holding the bottle up.

The same thought struck them simultaneously. Lisbie. There had been a time some months before, when she was having difficulties with a boyfriend, that she started drinking a lot more than she should have. Although alcohol had been forbidden until the girls were sixteen years old, both Jean and Steven had a fairly relaxed attitude to alcohol now that the girls were almost grown up. They both had a glass of wine when it was served at dinner, not every day, maybe a couple of times a week, and of course they went out with their friends to various social events where alcohol was consumed. But there was something different about this. Drinking a little with the family and friends was one thing, but secretly consuming substantial amounts was quite another.

"Is she home?" asked Steven, frowning.

"Yes, she's in her room . . ."

Steven, still holding the bottle, started toward the door with a determined step, but Jean said, "Not now, dear. May's with her—you remember May Gallacher, she's having dinner with us."

Steven turned and came back, took two Waterford sherry glasses off the tray, and started to pour into them.

At that moment the door opened and Lisbie came in with May, who was holding onto her hand.

Suddenly May started to cry, with tears rolling down her cheeks, and Steven, astonished, looked first at her, then at Lisbie.

"She's all right," said Lisbie, putting her arms around the girl. "She just does that sometimes, don't you, May? It just happens. It doesn't mean that she's sad, or anything."

"Would you like a little sherry?" Jean asked Lisbie, looking her straight in the eye. "You know that you're always welcome to have a wee drink, *as long as it's with us.*"

Lisbie went pink. "Yes, please," she said, but wouldn't look at either of them. Hiding his reluctance, Steven poured out a standard portion and handed Lisbie the glass.

"How about May?" he asked Jean quietly.

Jean shook her head. "No. For one thing, she's underage, and secondly, it wouldn't be good for her."

May, quite recovered from her brief crying spell, was looking around the room, but nothing seemed to be able to hold her attention. Her gaze moved from object to object without pausing, almost as if she didn't see them. She was so beautiful, thought Jean sadly, looking at her curly blond hair and rosy complexion, even with those vacant blue eyes and damaged brain.

"Would you like something?" Lisbie asked her. "Some orange juice?"

May turned to her, as if she were pulling herself back from far away, and shook her head. She smiled, took Lisbie's hand, and walked to the door.

" 'Bye!" said Lisbie, smiling back at her parents as she was pulled outside. A moment later Jean and Steven heard the two girls going back downstairs.

"Sad business," said Steven. "Poor kid."

"The spaghetti!" said Jean, putting her glass down hastily. "Come on through, Steven, dinner's just about ready."

Fiona came home a few moments later, and Jean, holding a wire basket full of steaming spaghetti, sent her up to see if her grandmother wanted to come down for dinner. "Don't forget to put on her slippers!" she called after her.

Everyone else had sat down when Mrs. Findlay

appeared, with Fiona behind her. Fiona rolled her eyes as if she'd had some difficulty convincing her grandmother to come down.

"Thanks for waiting for me!" snapped Mrs. Findlay at Jean, who, with a pile of plates in front of her, was just starting to serve.

"Do you remember May?" said Jean, in case her mother hadn't noticed the extra person at the table.

"Of course," replied Mrs. Findlay. She smiled at May, then looked back at Jean. "It's a pity none of your children are as pretty as she is."

"Gran!" said Fiona and Lisbie together, united in mock outrage.

With an unexpected, jerky movement of her arm, May accidentally knocked over her water glass, and in the resulting confusion Mrs. Findlay sat down primly in her usual chair next to Steven.

"I don't know how you put up with this disorder, day in and day out, Steven," she said to him in a voice pitched to be heard by Jean. "I know *my* husband wouldn't have tolerated it for one moment."

"Oh, it's all part of the fun of being a family," replied Steven airily, and Jean could have hugged him. "And I know you enjoy it as much as any of us." He smiled at Mrs. Findlay. He leaned over, sopped up a rivulet of water that was heading her way, and looked at Jean. He didn't wink, but it was there nevertheless. He came around the table and poured some Beaujolais into Jean's glass, and then into Mrs. Findlay's.

"I thought we were having *chicken*," she said pointedly.

"Well, I'm sorry, but I don't have any white wine, and this is better than nothing, right?" Steven's voice was still even, still friendly, but Jean could feel the edge on it, and she tensed. Her mother knew just how to get Steven to the point where he would leave the room in order to avoid further confrontation, and sometimes it seemed that Mrs. Findlay wanted to see how far she could push him.

Hurriedly, Jean filled up a plate and passed it to her mother, but when Mrs. Findlay leaned forward for it, the sleeve of her housecoat caught her wineglass and over it went, spilling a line of red wine across the white tablecloth, which was still wet from May's water. There was a moment's shocked silence, then Fiona and Lisbie exploded with uncontrollable laughter.

"It's just part of the fun of being a family!" Fiona just managed to say, and Lisbie, speechless, with tears of mirth running down her cheeks, almost finished up under the table. By the time order had been restored and Jean had emptied the saltcellar over the spilled wine, Mrs. Findlay was on her feet, her eyes flashing and her gnarled hands shaking with anger. "I've had enough of this," she said. "Those children . . ." She pointed a finger at Fiona, and then at Lisbie, then turned, almost lost her balance and leaned against the wall for a moment, then headed for the door. In the sudden quiet, they listened to her slow footsteps on the stairs. Jean sighed, and put her napkin on her bread plate. "I'll take her dinner up to her," she said. "Lisbie, May's not eating. Would you help her, please?"

Jean, carrying a tray, reached the top of the stairs about the same time as her mother. "I'm sorry, Mum," she said quietly. "You know how children are. I suppose we were the same when we were that age."

Mrs. Findlay didn't say anything until she was back in bed and Jean had put the tray on the bed table next to her. "Actually, you were worse," she said. "Your brothers were, anyway. Do you remember that time when we had that very proper French girl, Monique Levasseur, visiting, and at dinnertime Robert and Frank fell on each other with forks and knives, pretending to fight, and landed on the floor, just to take the Mickey out of her?"

Jean laughed, and sat at the end of the bed. "And you and Dad just went on eating and talking as if it happened all the time? I think it was that that got to her more than anything."

They chatted quietly for a few minutes, and when Jean felt that her mother had calmed down enough, she stood up. "I'd better get downstairs," she said. "Steven's tired, and the girls are on a roll down there. Is there anything else you need?"

"Well," replied Mrs. Findlay, looking at her plate, "I would like a little Beaujolais, if there's any left."

Chapter 12

Jean went back downstairs, feeling drained. She knew that every healthy family has occasional disagreements and squabbles, but still, it took a lot out of her, because she usually finished up somewhere in the middle. Maybe it was because by nature she was a participant rather than a mediator, she thought, trying to remember if lemon juice would help to get the wine stains out of the tablecloth.

She paused for a moment outside the dining room. The murmur of conversation sounded peaceful and unaggressive. With a quiet sigh of relief she went in and sat down at her place. Fiona had gathered up the plates, and Lisbie had passed out the dessert of fruit-flavored yogurt. Steven was trying to talk to May, but she couldn't pay attention to him for more than a moment, before her eyes would start looking blankly around the room.

The doorbell rang, and Fiona jumped up. "It's Douglas!" She ran to the door, and Jean could hear their voices in the corridor.

Douglas was looking somewhat subdued. He smiled at May and Lisbie, and nodded to Steven. Steven, who was scraping his spoon around to get what was left of the yogurt at the bottom of the container, nodded back, muttered something about having work to do, then stood up and left.

Douglas, used to the routine, took no offense, and sat down in Mrs. Findlay's chair.

"Would you like some coffee?" Fiona asked him, hovering around like a moth near a flame.

"Oh, for heaven's sake," muttered Lisbie, rolling her eyes at her mother.

"Yes, please," he replied. "With—"

"I know how you like it, Douglas," interrupted Fiona softly. "Milk and one sugar."

"I'm going to throw up," said Lisbie. "May, let's go downstairs." She stood up, took May's hand, and off they went.

"I'd like your advice, Jean," said Doug, speaking in a humble tone that irritated Jean beyond measure. "I'm not trying to involve you in this case, I promise, it's just there are some things I don't understand, things that with your medical knowledge . . ."

"Let's go into the living room, then," said Jean. "Fiona, would you please tidy up here? There's a new box of dishwashing powder on the counter."

"Okay." Fiona sounded resigned. It always seemed that when Douglas was visiting, her mother's only aim was to keep her away from him.

In the living room, Jean took her crochet out of its basket and sat down in her usual chair, feeling a bit guilty. She'd promised Hugh Kirkwall to do what she could to help him, but up to now, she hadn't been able to think of anything beyond giving him moral support. With Doug in the picture, she now had access to much more potentially helpful information.

Douglas started to pace up and down, but he caught Jean's glance and sat down in the green winged chair that he normally used. "The coroner's decided to label Robertson Kelso as a *suspicious death*," he said. "I hoped it would be *misadventure*, which is what they usually call this kind of hospital death. That would have got me off the hook."

"It's a conspiracy," smiled Jean. "They're ganging up on you."

Doug straightened up and stared at Jean for a moment. "Sometimes I suspect that you're pulling my leg, Jean. Other times I'm sure."

"Perish the thought." Jean shook her head. "If there's a conspiracy in this case, and maybe there is, I don't think it's against you."

Douglas nodded. "You mean it could be against Mr. Kirkwall? That Indian chap, Shah, certainly seems to have it in for him, doesn't he?"

"That's true," admitted Jean. "But that's not who I was thinking of. There are enough people out there who hated Robertson Kelso to make a small regiment."

"That Dr. Shah," went on Douglas, following his own train of thought, "could he have killed Kelso just to get Kirkwall in hot water? You know how those Orientals think—human life doesn't mean anything to them."

"Dr. Shah would be Asian, actually, wouldn't he?" murmured Jean. "And to me, anyway, he doesn't seem particularly bloodthirsty. Lots of sense of outrage, yes, and not much sense of humor, but I'd be surprised if he would do anything as . . . enterprising as killing a patient."

"He's called me already twice today to ask when I was going to arrest Mr. Kirkwall," said Douglas, sounding irritated. "Sandy Michie says Shah's the most persistent man he's ever met. And the most ambitious. Given half a chance, he'd take over the entire hospital."

Doug didn't say anything more for a few moments. He watched Jean working at her crochet, turning from time to time to a tattered piece of paper on which her pattern was apparently written.

"That postmortem . . ." he started, and Jean gave an involuntary shiver. "I don't understand what Dr. Anderson was talking about," he said. "How could there be no blood in his body if he didn't bleed after the operation was over, and there wasn't a bullet or a knife wound to let it out?"

"Douglas, I really don't know," said Jean, keeping her eyes on her work. She was telling the precise truth, although at least one horrifying possibility had occurred to her.

Douglas hesitated. "You know that in the last few weeks there's been a lot of talk around the area about strange occurrences . . . There was that young woman near Blairgowrie who was found dying in the alley behind her house. I don't know it for a fact, but the paper said the only mark on her was . . . on her neck. And there have been others, not just humans. Like those two heifers on the Strathalmond estate that were found dead . . ."

"Come on, Douglas, you're not suggesting that there are vampires at work here in Scotland, are you?" said Jean, looking up. She smiled at him. "Don't be so silly."

Douglas blushed a bright pink. "All right then," he said, annoyed. "*You* tell me how it happened. Dr. Anderson doesn't have any scientific answers, and nor does anybody else I've talked to, so if the standard explanations don't work, you have to look elsewhere, right?"

"Not really, Douglas. I'm not saying there's a scientific explanation for everything, because of course there isn't; but in situations like this, there usually is one. Just because we don't understand the mechanics of a gruesome situation such as Kelso's death, it doesn't necessarily mean we have to look for supernatural events to explain what's happened."

Douglas shrugged, still annoyed. "You still haven't given me an answer," he said.

"Douglas, I don't have one. Maybe . . ." A thought crossed her mind. "Did you talk to Mrs. Kelso yet?"

"Not yet," he replied. "She went up to visit her

mother in Buckie, and she won't be back until tomorrow."

Jean hesitated; it was always difficult, weighing patient confidentiality against disclosures that were occasionally necessary to protect others.

"I suggested to Malcolm Anderson that he might want to check Kelso's tissues for insulin," she said, speaking carefully.

Douglas stared at her. "Insulin? Was he diabetic?"

"No, Douglas, he was not," replied Jean with emphasis. "And as you're one person for whom I don't have to cross every *t* or dot every *i*, I'm not saying anything more about it."

Douglas thought about it for a moment. "All right," he said, "I understand. I think. How long will it take Dr. Anderson to get the insulin test back?"

"Maybe tomorrow. It depends on how busy the lab is. He said he'd let me know as soon as he heard."

The doorbell rang, and one of the girls must have answered, because a murmur of voices was heard in the hallway outside.

"That's May's mother," said Jean listening. She went to the door and opened it. "Rosemary!" she said. "Come in, come in." She turned to Fiona. "Would you like to make some tea for us all, dear?"

Rosemary came into the living room, and Douglas stood up.

"You know Douglas Niven, don't you?"

"Yes, of course. We all go to St. John's Church." Rosemary smiled at Douglas. "How's Cathie? I didn't see her on Sunday."

"She was busy with the bairn," replied Douglas. "He had a bad earache over the weekend, so she stayed home with him."

"That's a shame, the poor wee lad," said Rosemary sympathetically. "Is he over it now?"

"Aye, he's fine now." Douglas smiled proudly. "It takes more than just a little earache to keep him down for long."

"The girls are downstairs," Jean told Rosemary. "They seem to be having a good time together."

"Lisbie's so sweet with May," said Rosemary, looking gratefully at Jean. "Your daughter is a very wonderful young woman."

"Thank you, Rosemary. Actually, Doug and I were talking about Robertson Kelso just now," said Jean, clearing a place on the table for when Fiona came back with the tea tray.

"Yes . . ." Rosemary's calm eyes went from Jean to Doug. "That was certainly a surprise when he died, wasn't it?"

"The surprise for most people seemed to be the *way* he died," said Doug. "Actually, I was going to ask you about that, Rosemary, as you were on duty," said Douglas, relieved that he could talk to her in these unofficial surroundings, and also that Jean was here with him.

"I was expecting to hear from you," said Rosemary, smiling in her self-contained, almost prim way. She sat down on the piano stool between

Doug and Jean, and folded her hands in her lap. "Especially after all the fuss that Dr. Shah's making about it up at the hospital."

"I hardly know where to begin," confessed Doug. "You see, I feel that some people have been putting up smoke screens here. What I mean is that, quite aside from Kelso himself, certain people seem to be either attacking or trying to protect others. For instance"—Doug moved in his chair—"you mentioned Dr. Shah. He seems to have some kind of bitter antagonism against Mr. Kirkwall, and from the sounds of it, he's using this whole incident to try to pin him to the wall."

"That's been going on for quite a while," said Rosemary. "Dr. Shah is very pushy, in a, well"— she glanced at Jean, as if to get her permission to divulge industry secrets—"in a *slimy* kind of way. He wants to be in charge of the important hospital committees, and he knows that in the normal way he wouldn't stand a chance. So he thinks that if he can come across as the new broom who sweeps away laziness and incompetence, he'll get there. But, of course, Mr. Kirkwall is in his way. Everybody likes Mr. Kirkwall, and yes, they try to protect him."

"You, too?"

Rosemary paused. "Yes, I suppose I have," she said. "It was so sad, what happened to Mr. Kirkwall. They were such a nice couple, him and Frances, until that Kelso came on the scene. He was one of those men with an instinct for picking out vulnerable women, and he knew just when to strike. And so there he was, ready and waiting when Frances was having problems with Hugh."

Rosemary's usually stolid face had gone pink with the intensity of her feeling, and Jean watched her with some surprise. One could never tell what went on behind people's eyes, she thought, or know how deeply events affected them. Rosemary was not finished, though. "And Hugh had been so good, before that," she went on, "he was certainly the best surgeon in Perth, and then . . . well, when he started drinking too much, we all thought it would be a passing thing, and we tried to help him through these bad times, thinking that he'd eventually get over it." Rosemary sighed at the admission, and looked at the floor. She had certainly misjudged that situation, and knew it.

"So what happened this time, when Kelso was admitted?"

"Well, first Dr. Shah saw him in the emergency room, and called Mr. Kirkwall. Kelso was too ill to be sent anywhere else—he had to be taken care of here. And there was a bit of a delay before Mr. Kirkwall got to the hospital."

"Do you think Mr. Kirkwall knew who the patient was? I mean, before the doctor got to the hospital?"

"I'm sure he didn't. He'd have insisted we send him to Dundee, however sick Kelso was. We all think that was a deliberate dirty trick on Shah's part, not telling him. But, once Mr. Kirkwall had actually seen him, he was forced to take care of him, and that of course meant operating."

"Now, Rosemary, among friends, and between these four walls, do you think that Mr. Kirkwall might have deliberately done something that . . ." Douglas didn't know quite which words to use. "That might have resulted in Kelso's death?"

Rosemary nodded as if she'd been asking herself the same question. "No," she said firmly, "I don't. He's not the type. Obviously, he hated Kelso for what he'd done, but once he was a patient, he would do everything he could for him. And anyway, Mr. Kirkwall isn't a surreptitious person. He wouldn't do something like that secretly. I don't think so, anyway."

"Also if he'd done anything to kill him, or even to hasten his death, it would have reflected on his professional skills," said Jean, who had been listening carefully. "And as the operation itself hadn't gone too smoothly, it would have been asking for trouble if he had done anything in addition. Especially as he knew that Dr. Shah would be out there waiting to pounce."

The door opened, and Fiona came in with a loaded tray, and the next few moments were filled with the quiet tinkling of cups and setting out of plates with slices of fruitcake and chocolate biscuits.

Fiona saw that the conversation didn't concern her, and for once didn't try to stay. But, as she left the room, she couldn't resist walking around the table and brushing quite accidentally against Doug's arm.

"You must be very proud of your girls, Jean,"

said Rosemary, balancing a chocolate biscuit carefully on the rim of her saucer so that it wouldn't melt against the hot cup.

"We've been lucky, I suppose," replied Jean. "When you think of what some kids get up to these days ..." She blushed, embarrassed for a moment, and turned to Douglas. "Sugar and milk?" she asked, temporarily flustered, although she knew perfectly well how he took his tea.

"Yes, please." Douglas watched Jean curiously as she poured in the milk.

It's a funny thing about Douglas, she thought. He certainly has the antennae to detect when something's happening, but usually he doesn't know enough about the situation or the circumstances to figure it out and put it all together.

"Now, where were we?" he asked Jean. "Aye, you both agreed that Mr. Kirkwall wouldn't be likely to have killed Robertson Kelso."

"Actually, Douglas, nobody's proved that *anyone* killed Robertson Kelso," Jean pointed out. "Dr. Anderson said that one possibility was an unexplained postoperative heart failure. They do occur from time to time."

"Well, I suppose so," replied Douglas, taking a sip of tea, "but that's not what the coroner thought. Now, Rosemary," he went on, turning to her, "tell me what happened after the operation was over."

"Well, he seemed to be doing all right, so they decided to put him back in his room rather than into intensive care," replied Rosemary. "So we took him up to his room, put him in bed, and made sure his vital signs were all right. Then Mr. Kirkwall went down to the waiting room and brought Mrs. Kelso back.''

"What time was that, Rosemary?"

"Oh, it must have been somewhere around ten o'clock,'' she replied. "Because the operation was over at about a quarter to.''

"Who was taking care of him at that time?"

"For the first hour or so it was the nurse on evenings, John McDonald. Then at eleven Mona Jennings came on. I stayed on for the night shift, and I came up, oh, every couple of hours or so to keep an eye on things. Mona's all right, but she's quite a bit older, and isn't always as aware of problems as some of the others.''

"At what time did Mrs. Kelso leave?"

"It must have been sometime between midnight and one. When I stopped in at one, she'd already gone.''

"And did Kelso seem all right then?"

Rosemary hesitated. "He was asleep, or anyway he seemed asleep. I checked his pulse and his breathing, and these were all right, so I didn't try to waken him.''

"Is it easy to tell the difference between normal sleep and, for instance, a coma?''

Rosemary thought for a moment. "Well, when they're in a coma, their sleep is often noisy; they grunt and rattle, and, of course it's deeper than normal sleep, and you can't rouse them. It's sort of hard to describe, but when you've been around as long as I have, you can usually tell the difference."

"So you saw him at one o'clock. When did you check on him again?"

"Around three. We had a problem in the ICU, a heart attack, so I came up after that was sorted out."

"Was he okay then?"

"I think so. He seemed just about the same, so I didn't spend more than a minute there with him."

"Was nurse Jennings with you? When you went to see him?"

Rosemary gave a short sigh. "Yes, she was," she replied. "Nurse Jennings was actually having a little nap in her chair when I came up, but she soon woke up, I can assure you. She came with me to Kelso's room, and I made her check his pulse and blood pressure."

"You said that was all normal."

"Yes."

"Did you see him again, after that?"

"No I didn't. There was an accident on the Dundee Road with a carload of football fans coming home late, so I was kept pretty busy up to the time I went off. And I was really tired, having done a double shift, so I just went off home."

"Did you see Mr. Kirkwall when he came in that morning?"

"No. That must have been after I went off duty."

Douglas was running out of questions. "Did

you see anyone else around? Anybody who might have gone into his room?"

Again, Rosemary hesitated, and her honest face showed the difficulty she was experiencing. "Well, yes," she said slowly. "Although I didn't actually see him in the room."

"And who might that have been?" In spite of himself, Doug was reverting to his ponderous police-speak, and Jean smiled invisibly, although she was as interested as he was to hear who Rosemary was talking about.

"You know Doris Caie, Jean?" asked Rosemary, who seemed to be looking to her for some kind of support. Jean nodded, but when she realized the significance of the question, she put her hand up to her mouth and said, very quietly, "Oh, no!"

"Are you talking about Ms. Caie, the emergency room nurse?" asked Doug stiffly. He could see that they knew something he didn't, and it annoyed him that once again his ignorance of local matters and people had left him out of the loop.

"Yes. Doris Caie is the senior evening nurse in the emergency room," said Rosemary, but that didn't tell Doug very much.

Jean decided to fill in the gaps for him. "You probably don't remember the story of her husband, Albert Caie, who was Robertson Kelso's principal accountant for a while. Well, I don't know all the details, but Albert and Kelso had a big falling out. Soon after that, Albert's office was broken into, all his records were destroyed, including Kelso's, and Kelso sued him for negligence, and put out stories that Albert had embezzled lots of his money. Then Albert was attacked in broad daylight and had both his legs broken. He got better, but he couldn't prove that Kelso was responsible, and was ruined financially. Doris had to go back to work as a nurse, and happened to be on duty the evening Kelso came in."

"You saw this man Caie, Rosemary? That night in the hospital?" Doug's voice was calm, but his eyes had lit up, and he sat very straight in the chair.

"Yes, just before eleven. He was walking along the main corridor, away from the emergency room when I came down the stairs," she said. "He saw me and ducked into the men's room. I was on my way to Emergency, and I mentioned to Doris that I'd seen him, and she seemed very uncomfortable, almost alarmed. She said she was just going off duty and he'd come to pick her up. But he didn't reappear, and a little while later I saw Doris, with her overcoat on, going out to the staff car park. But there was no sign of Albert. I was busy at the time, and didn't think anything about it. I assumed he'd already gone out and was waiting for her out in the car."

"I thought you said you'd seen him in Kelso's room," said Douglas, sounding a little disappointed.

"No. But later I did see somebody who looked a lot like him up on the fourth floor, where Kelso's room was. Albert limps, and that night he was wearing a raincoat, and so was this person I saw hanging around. He disappeared into the stairwell at the end of the corridor when I came along. But of course it could have been somebody coming out of the intensive care waiting room. There were lots of people up there that night."

Douglas sighed. This case was getting more complicated every time he tried to tie up the loose ends. "And what time might that have occurred, Rosemary? When you bumped into this limping man with the raincoat?"

"I didn't bump into him, Douglas," replied Rosemary patiently. "He was a good fifty feet away from me, and the lights were dim, on night standby. I really didn't get a good look at him."

"Time?"

"About one, I suppose . . . Yes, that's right, a bit before one, because I was on my way to see Kelso."

"And you'd seen Caie at about eleven? The first time?"

Rosemary nodded.

"So he must have been hanging around somewhere in the hospital for two hours? Wouldn't he have been spotted long before?"

"Not necessarily. Most of the hospital is dark at night, the staff is down to a bare minimum, and there are lots of places a person could hide, like treatment rooms, toilets, or broom cupboards."

"What did you do? I mean, about the man?"

"I phoned down to Andy McKaig, the security

guard, and he said he'd keep an eye out for him, but I don't know if he ever did see him."

"You saw Kelso after that, right? So if this Caie chap had actually done something to Kelso while he was up on the fourth floor, you would have known about it?"

Rosemary agreed, but she didn't seem quite convinced, and Jean resolved to talk to her about it at some other time.

There was a giggling noise outside the door, and a moment later Lisbie and May came in. Good-byes were said, and everyone went their respective ways. Jean stopped Lisbie as she was about to go to her room, took her arm, and led her gently back into the living room, where she sat her down in the green chair that Doug had been sitting in.

"Lisbie," she said, taking her daughter's hand and looking into her eyes with profound concern. "What's the matter, dear? Is there something bad happening to you?"

Lisbie pulled her hand away. "No, of course not," she said, her voice suddenly defensive. "I'm fine. Why?"

"Well," said Jean, trying to sound as supportive as she could, "about a year ago, do you remember, you were having a problem with the boy you were seeing, Dave . . ."

"Don't even mention his name," said Lisbie. "I hate him." She stood up. "Mum, I'm tired, and I'm going to bed."

"Lisbie, sit down, please." On the rare occasions

Jean spoke in that tone, she was obeyed instantly, and Lisbie dropped back down on the chair as if her legs had suddenly vanished from under her. "The reason I mentioned Dave was because that was when you started dipping into the sherry," Jean went on. "And so I'm wondering what's happening now."

"Dave had nothing whatever to do with it," said Lisbie. "I . . . anyway, I stopped, didn't I? Taking the sherry?"

"Yes, you did."

There was a silence for a few moments, then Lisbie tried to speak. Her eyes were shining with tears, and she could barely get her words out. "It's May," she said. "I feel so bad about her. Her mum and dad are always talking about how she used to be, before her accident. They have albums and albums of photos, videos of her at school, winning races, at the prize givings. And now poor May, she can't do anything, she can't even put on her clothes properly by herself, and she doesn't understand anything. She's so pretty and sweet, and I can't do anything to help, and it makes me so sad just to look at her. . . ."

They talked about May for a few minutes longer. Jean asked Lisbie if it might not be better to stop seeing her, or at least less often, and Lisbie refused indignantly.

"Then, don't look back," said Jean, who had expected that response. "Don't think or hope that May can go back to who she was. Remember, you have a different perspective from her parents, because you didn't even know her then. Now May's a different person from what she was, with certain needs that you enjoy helping her with. But she's not unhappy, and she has a life. It's different from yours, but not something you should be sad about. She loves you, and you make her happy. Enjoy the pleasure of it, and look forward rather than back."

Lisbie thought about her mother's words, and the more she thought about them, the more they made sense. They talked for a couple of minutes, then Lisbie stood up, kissed her mother, and went off to bed.

Jean worked on her crochet a little longer, then stood up, feeling a bit stiff, and went quickly around the house putting out lights, closing doors, and straightening chairs. Then she locked the front door, checked the back door, and went slowly up the stairs to bed. At the top of the stairs, she paused for a moment. Her mother was snoring audibly, and Jean thought sadly of the time in the future when there would be no sounds of life from that room.

She crept into bed, trying not to wake Steven, and lay awake for a long time, thinking first about May and her parents, then about Robertson Kelso's death. If it had been anyone else, she thought, it would have been considered an accident and treated as such. But because it *was* Robertson Kelso, such considerations had been put aside, partly as a result of Dr. Shah's prodding, but also because so many people were known to want him dead.

In her mind, Jean went through the list of possible suspects, although she was well aware that there might be others she knew nothing about. Dr. Shah, of course, was using Kelso's death to further his own ambitions, and everyone knew he despised and detested Hugh Kirkwall, who had humiliated him and stood in the way of his professional advancement. Could Shah have somehow carried out, or arranged Kelso's death in order to destroy Hugh Kirkwall? Shah certainly hadn't wasted any time in taking advantage of the situation, almost as if he'd premeditated the entire incident. But he hadn't had any more warning of Kelso's illness than anyone else. Could he have poisoned Kelso? Shah, trained in India, could have knowledge of all kinds of vegetable poisons that were unknown in the West and virtually untraceable even with modern laboratory techniques. It was at least theoretically possible, Jean thought, even if it sounded a bit melodramatic.

Who else? What about Albert Caie? Was he the person Rosemary had seen skulking around on the fourth floor of the hospital? He certainly had enough reason to want Kelso dead. And if he wasn't there with criminal intent, what was he doing there in the hospital?

Jean sighed, and Steven stirred in his sleep, turned on his side, and put one arm across her. She held onto his arm, feeling the weight of it on her body, and deriving a reassuring sense of security from his solid presence and warmth next to her.

How about Rosemary herself? Rosemary was one of those solid, trustworthy, sensible people who never panicked, who was always reliable in an emergency. It was hard to imagine her creeping around the hospital with homicidal intent. And, as far as Jean knew, there was no reason why Rosemary would have any particular bone to pick with Robertson Kelso. But one never knew for sure—Jean resolved to think some more about that. Perth was a small town, and Jean had an uncanny ability to find things out when she wanted to.

One of the people no one had seemed to take very seriously was Irene, Kelso's wife. Maybe it was because she was such a sad, mousy little person who went her own silent way, without friends or relatives, nursing her bruises, trying ineffectively to protect her son Jeff from his father's brutality. The only time anyone saw her was when she went shopping in town, scuttling unobtrusively from one shop to the next, scarfed head down. But Irene hadn't always been like that. She had been a pretty, vivacious girl who'd worked as an assistant manager in one of Kelso's new fish-growing factories. He'd been so nice to her, so gentle and considerate in his courtship, that she ignored her friends' warnings and eventually married him.

It hadn't lasted long. At first it was only verbal abuse, as he taunted her with her lack of schooling, the poverty of her intellectual resources. And he hadn't wanted the baby, which made things worse between them. And it had only been a matter of weeks before he was back to his philandering again.

Jean forced her mind back to the present. Would Irene have had the guts to kill the man who had persecuted her and her child? Jean knew enough about battered women and about Irene in particular, to know that the answer was yes. And Irene had access to insulin, and probably knew that a large insulin injection would be quite enough to kill a man, especially in a postoperative state where he wasn't getting anything to eat or drink. And, of course, there was the money. Kelso had been rich, and presumably all his wealth would pass on to Irene and Jeff. That thought really made her pause. Sadly enough, money had been at the root of many of the cases she'd worked on with Douglas Niven, and that fact alone would put Irene at or near the top of any list of suspects.

But, strangely enough, as she lay quietly in bed, hearing the occasional city noise, the faint whine of a distant ambulance siren, and the big old horse-chestnut branches creaking in the wind outside, the one who worried Jean the most was Hugh Kirkwall himself. Driven to drink by his wife's desertion, and suddenly having in his power the man who had been responsible for his misery . . . It was hard to ignore the possibility that he had had something to do with Kelso's death. Of course, he had asked for Jean's help, but that, she recognized, could have been a ploy to deflect her suspicions. Jean could feel the blood pounding between her temples, and tried to settle herself for sleep. Steven was snoring gently, but it didn't bother her. On the contrary, it was audible proof that he was alive and *there*. She kissed him gently on the side of his neck, and turned over on her side.

The last thing Jean remembered thinking about was if Kelso had, in fact, been killed, how had it been done? That seemed to be the basic and so far unanswered question that lay at the core of the entire case.

Chapter 13

Next morning, Douglas and Jamieson drove to the Kelso estate, about eight miles out of town along the Islay Road, past Scone Palace, and beyond the road that led up to Strathalmond Castle, near where, some months before, Graeme Ferguson had met his grisly death. Douglas, who was driving, saw the turnoff to the Kelso estate too late, but nevertheless he swung the wheel around and with a protesting squeal of tires, the car slid sideways into the narrow secondary road, went up onto the verge, kicking up a cloud of dust and weeds. Douglas gunned the motor and spun the rear wheels to get the car turned faster, the way he'd been taught at the defensive driving school. Jamieson, who had closed his eyes when he saw what Doug was about to do, held on tightly to the crash-handle mounted on the dashboard, and winced at the sound of the car scraping along the side of the hawthorn hedge. When Jamieson opened his eyes some thirty seconds later, Douglas was proceeding in a perfectly decorous fashion up the road.

"Glad there was nothing coming the other way," said Jamieson when he got his breath back. He tried to keep his voice steady and unreproachful.

"Och, there's never any traffic on this road," replied Douglas calmly.

Half a mile farther, they came to a big open gate with great pots of bright red geraniums on each side, and the road surface changed from macadam to gravel. Douglas slowed down, thinking that coming to a stop at the Kelsos' house in a skidding flurry of flying gravel might not convey the impression of calm official grief and sympathy that he wished to present to Irene Kelso.

The Kelso residence was modern and imposing, with lots of glass separated by heavy slabs of gray concrete partially hidden by a wall backed with dark green cedars. Between the driveway and the heavy, carved oak front door was a glass geodesic dome supported by four slim steel pillars. This dome covered a small formal garden, with rosebushes on each side of a tiled pathway. Externally, the house resembled an unhealthy collaboration between Buckminster Fuller and Frank Lloyd Wright, although to Doug it seemed merely an expression of arrogant wealth, built with money torn by a rapacious plutocrat from the slender wallets of the poor.

"I wouldn't mind a place like this," said Jamieson, looking around as they walked toward the front door.

Douglas snorted. "Huh," he said. "On a policeman's salary? You're out of your mind!" He took a deep breath, and launched into one of his left-leaning tirades. "Get it into your head, my boy, you and I, we're close to the bottom of the social and economic . . ." His words trailed off when the door opened to reveal Irene Kelso with her son, Jeff. He was standing next to her, partly hidden by her skirts, looking wide-eyed and terrified as the two men walked along the short, rose-lined walk toward them.

"Mrs. Kelso?" Doug introduced himself and Jamieson. Irene was wearing a long black skirt of some cheap material, and a shapeless turtleneck sweater with long sleeves. Doug looked at her dull eyes and battered features, now covered with pinkish makeup, and tried to imagine how she had reacted while her husband had been beating her up. Did she fight back? Did she cower in a corner? Did she scream, or suffer in silence?

"Jeff thinks you've come to take him away," said Irene, looking anxiously down at her son. She put a protective arm around him. "Please tell him that you're not."

"We won't take him away unless he's done something very bad," said Jamieson in his ponderous voice, making a feeble attempt at humor.

Jeff looked even more scared, and disappeared completely behind his mother's skirts.

"No, sonny, we're not coming to take you away. We've just come to talk to your mum for a wee while," said Doug, smiling at Jeff, and wondering how his son, Douglas Jr., would look at this age. He fished in his pocket and pulled out a cellophane-wrapped restaurant mint. "Here," he said, holding it out to Jeff, who glanced up at his mother, then shook his head.

"Come in, please," said Irene in her flat, expressionless voice. She patted her son on the head. "Jeff, off you go and play with your toy soldiers. It'll just be a few minutes."

Douglas and Jamieson followed Irene through a big tiled open area with an ornate Italian fountain in the middle, into a large room with a varnished hardwood floor and almost no furnishings. There was no carpet, and three easy chairs huddled at the end of the room around a big fireplace. Against the wall, opposite a French door that led out to the garden, stood a plain deal table with a lamp, some magazines, and a telephone.

"Robertson didn't like the house cluttered up," said Irene, catching Doug's surprised. Their footsteps clattered on the bare boards as they crossed the room.

"Please have a seat," she said.

Douglas moved one of the chairs slightly to form a triangle. Irene slumped down in one of them, looking very tired, her hands in her lap. Douglas noticed that although she seemed outwardly calm enough, her fingers were twisting together. She saw him looking so she put her hands together and held them tightly between her knees.

"We're not going to keep you very long, Mrs. Kelso," said Douglas sympathetically. "But I'm sure you understand that, under the circumstances, we have to ask you a few questions."

Irene nodded. Douglas thought that her eyes didn't seem to look quite in the same direction.

"After Mr. Kirkwall brought you up to your husband's hospital room, after the operation," he started, "was there anybody else there with you?"

"No." Irene shook her head. A straggly piece of dark hair came over her face, and she pushed it back with a listless movement.

"Who else came in to the room after you were there?"

"The night nurse. It was a man. He checked Rob's pulse and did that stuff with the armband. His blood pressure, or something like that."

"What was his name?"

"I don't know. I didn't ask."

"Anybody else?"

"Only the doctor who put him to sleep. A nice lady ... Dr. Anna Mc ... I don't remember."

"McKenzie?"

"Yes. I think so."

"And what did she do?"

"She examined him, listened to his chest, shone a light in his eyes. Then she gave him an injection—in his arm. It just took a second."

Douglas sat up straight, and glanced over to make sure Jamieson was taking notes. "An injection? What kind of injection?"

"I don't know. She didn't say."

"What *did* she say?"

"She said it was to help his breathing, or something like that. I don't know. They all speak in those medical terms, and I don't know what they're talking about."

"Was he awake or asleep at that time?"

"Asleep. He didn't even move with the injection."

"Did he wake up while you were there?"

"No. He grunted a couple of times, and started to make a snoring noise about twenty minutes after she'd gone, but he didn't wake up."

"Didn't the night nurse come in again?"

"No." Irene looked up. "When I left, he'd gone, and there was a new one at the nurses' desk with her head down on her arms. She was making more noise than Rob, with her snoring."

"And about what time was it that you left, Mrs. Kelso?"

"Oh, it must have been about one in the morning. I was really tired and needed to go home. And there wasn't anything for me to do."

"Ah." Douglas said nothing for a moment, then raised his head and looked through the wide window into the garden. Between the huge old ash trees that dotted the grounds, a beautifully kept lawn stretched gently down to the banks of the Tay. "I assume you'll now own all this," he said, waving a hand to include the house and the land. "Plus the fish farms and whatever else."

"It'll be all held in trust for Jeff," she said, showing for the first time a hint of sparkle. "The trustee is the Royal Bank of Scotland. Personally, I don't want anything. I have a bit of money of my own, not much, but I want to get a job again."

She looked at her surroundings with an expression of disgust. "If you knew how much lying and cheating Robertson did to get this, and all the other stuff . . ."

"Did you see Albert Caie that night?" asked Douglas in a suddenly abrupt voice. He stared hard at her. "Did he come into Mr. Kelso's room?"

Irene was caught off guard, as Doug had intended, and her face turned a blotchy, unattractive color. She put her head down. "Why do you ask? Why should he have been there?"

"He *was* there, and came into the room, didn't he, Mrs. Kelso?" Doug raised his voice, and she quailed. Instinctively, Doug knew how she would respond to bullying or threats—that was why some women remained in that kind of abusive situation. Jamieson moved in his chair, and his face reddened angrily at his boss for yelling at this poor little maltreated woman.

Irene cowered, and half raised a defensive arm, as if afraid that Doug would strike her. But she didn't say anything.

Doug stood up. "Well?" he said, coming closer to her, his whole posture threatening.

"Yes, he did come in," she said breathlessly. "I told him to leave. He had a gun in his pocket and took it out. He was shaking so much I thought he might kill me, or himself, by accident."

"So what happened?" asked Douglas in a much quieter tone, feeling rather complacent that his hunch had paid off.

"He stuck the gun in the back of Robertson's

neck, and held it there. I told him to stop or I'd scream, and then he ... well, he finally put the gun back in the pocket of his raincoat. Then ... then he started to cry."

Douglas was about to ask something, then decided that he would probably get more information by keeping quiet and listening.

Sure enough, Irene went on. "Then he just stood there, crying, making a harsh, awful kind of noise. I'd never heard anything like it before. I knew what Albert had been through, and the terrible things that Robertson had done to him. I stood up and hugged him for a minute. Then he almost ran out of the room. He didn't say a single word all the time he was there."

For a long moment no one said anything. Both Doug and Jamieson were visualizing the scene.

"Mrs. Kelso, I want you to think very carefully before you answer my next question. Did you inject insulin or any other substance into your husband at any time while you were with him at the hospital?"

Irene raised her head and for the first time, it seemed, looked directly at Douglas. "No I didn't," she said. "I can't say it didn't cross my mind, but I didn't do it." Maybe because only half her face smiled, to Douglas her expression seemed bitter, almost demented. "If Albert Caie hadn't come in, maybe I would have."

Douglas and Jamieson left the Kelso home soon after; Irene had become very tired and seemed to have nothing more of importance to tell them.

"Do you think she's lying?" Douglas asked Jamieson as they got into the car.

Jamieson didn't answer immediately; he was strapping himself in with ostentatious care for the return trip. "No, sir," he said, hiding his reproach. "She was too afraid of you, especially when you started shouting at her. She was too scared to lie."

"She may not be lying," said Douglas, "but she knows something about this business that she isn't telling. She wouldn't have said anything about Albert Caie, either, if we hadn't got it out of her."

"*You* got it out of her, sir. All I did was take notes." Jamieson spoke as if he were preparing for a hostile intradepartmental investigation.

"Whatever." Douglas put his foot on the accelerator as soon as the gravel drive became a paved road, but there was still enough gravel to send it flying in a burst behind the car, making a noise like a machine gun when the granite chips struck the underside of the vehicle. "And all that stuff about not wanting anything for herself, it's all in trust for Jeff . . . Did that sound right to you, too?"

"Yes, sir, it did. She sounds as though she had been a fine woman before being broken by her sadistic husband."

"For God's sake, Jamieson, you sound like the back cover of a cheap thriller," said Douglas, paying no attention to the stop sign at the main road. Luckily, there was no traffic, and Douglas swung wide around the corner and settled down for a fast ride home. Jamieson, who had cringed down as the stop sign approached at an unnerving speed, slid back up.

"If we'd hit something back there," said Douglas, "that seat belt would have caught you around the neck and killed you. Sit up straight in the future, okay?"

"Yes, sir. I'll be happy to drive if you prefer, sir."

Douglas wasn't listening. "When we talked to Dr. Anna McKenzie, did she say anything about giving Kelso an injection after the operation?"

"No, sir, she didn't."

"Well, I think maybe we should talk to her again." There was a silence while Douglas swung out behind and passed a bus slowing for the entrance to Scone Palace. Coming the other way on the two-lane road was a large lorry, and Jamieson closed his eyes and forced himself to stay upright in his seat. He can't force me to keep my eyes open, he thought angrily. A couple of sharp swerves later, Jamieson opened his eyes and the road was magically clear again.

"She seemed to have a thing going for Mr. Kirkwall, didn't you think?" asked Douglas.

"Who . . . ?"

"Dr. Anna McKenzie. Pay attention when I'm talking to you, Jamieson. She was very protective of Mr. Kirkwall when we talked to her. Maybe she's in love with him, and knowing what Kelso had done to him, stealing his wife and all, she was in the best position of anybody to kill him, to revenge her lover."

"You're the one who's sounding like a back cover now," said Jamieson, taking a chance.

"Maybe we've been looking in the wrong direction," went on Douglas, oblivious to Jamieson's comment. "Maybe it was insulin, but it could have been Dr. McKenzie who gave it."

"Maybe all those people who hated Kelso got together," suggested Jamieson. "Like in that Agatha Christie story where somebody gets killed on a train . . ." His voice faded as Douglas turned the corner from Bridgend onto the old Tay bridge into town, narrowly missing an elderly man on a bicycle.

"We're going back up to the hospital," said Douglas, his eyes gleaming. "First we're going to have a wee chat with that nurse, Doris Caie, and then we'll talk to Dr. Anna McKenzie again. Jamieson, I have a feeling that we're finally getting closer to a solution."

Chapter 14

At the surgery, Jean was between patients, and taking a quick cup of tea with her old partner, Helen Inkster, who, a few months before, had come back to help out after the death of Jean's assistant, Diane Taggart.

"Did you see today's paper?" asked Helen in her deep voice. She was a big, rawboned woman who invariably wore tweeds, thick lisle stockings, and shoes suitable for winter trudging in the Apennines.

"No." Jean shook her head. She was opening the foil wrapper on a Penguin chocolate biscuit, and trying to read a pathology report from the Dundee labs at the same time.

"Well, you should take a glance at it," said Helen in a voice that made Jean look up. Helen proffered the *Journal*, folded in half. Jean put down the Penguin and opened the paper.

" 'Mystery Death at Hospital,' " she read. " 'Well-known area businessman dies after minor operation.' " The story went on to say that a hospital investigation was in progress, and that "attempts had been made to contact controversial surgeon Mr. Hugh Kirkwall, but he was not available for comment."

"Oh, dear," said Jean when she finished reading the story. "Poor Hugh. Talk about trial by the press. They're making it look very bad for him."

"I'm surprised that Sandy Michie allowed anybody at the hospital to talk to the press," said Helen, watching Jean.

"He didn't. Hugh told me Michie had forbidden the staff to talk to anyone about the case." She paused, her eyes still on the paper. "He's not mentioned by name, but I'm afraid this article has Dr. Shah's signature written all over it."

"That awful man!" said Helen, with unusual vehemence. "Do you remember the old days when doctors stuck together, and supported each other when there was trouble?"

"Yes I do," said Jean. "And I think that most of us still feel that way. Except, of course, when someone's done something that's clearly in the wrong."

"Maybe this is such a case." Helen shrugged, annoyed. "But it still doesn't excuse Shah from anonymously pointing a finger at Mr. Kirkwall like that. He doesn't *know* that Kirkwall did anything wrong. Nobody does, from the sounds of it."

The door opened, and Eleanor poked her head into the room. "Telephone, Dr. Jean," she said. "It's Dr. Anderson."

Jean put down her cup and hurried into her office.

Dr. Anderson's voice was brisk as ever, but it held a trace of anxiety that he couldn't hide. "The toxicology report came back on Kelso," he said. "The only thing they found were traces of the anesthetic and muscle relaxants, in amounts consistent with normal use of these drugs. There was no trace of insulin. Or anything else, for that matter."

"Malcolm, are all poisons picked up by this chemical screening system?"

"Well, not by this system we have here. They tell me some of the new American analyzers pick up more than ours can. Some vegetable toxins, for instance . . . But most of the ordinary ones show up."

"Maybe we're dealing with a non-ordinary one."

"Yes. That's why I sent a second sample to the central toxicology lab in Hammersmith. That's the one Scotland Yard uses to check on their own results, so it should be okay." Malcolm Anderson had always been skeptical of anything south of the border, and it showed in his voice.

"When will you hear from them?"

"In a few days, I hope. But you know how slow those Sassenachs are anyway, and as it's only for a Scottish hospital, our samples go automatically to the end of the line."

"Oh, dear." Jean pondered for a moment. "Do you have any more ideas about how Kelso died?"

Anderson sighed. "I've been beating my brains

over this one, quine, and I haven't come up with anything. If the toxicologists come up empty-handed, I'm afraid we're stuck. It's not often that I don't come up with enough findings to establish an exact cause of death, I can tell you that much, but with this one . . . I spent hours in the library, trying to find some answers, and I've phoned my colleagues in Edinburgh and Glasgow, but they didn't have any helpful suggestions. Not that they've *ever* been that much use to me, if the truth be known."

"The coroner doesn't seem to think that it was an accidental death."

"Ach, Jean, what does he know?" Anderson's voice rose with frustration. "That chap's just a retired lawyer. All he knows is what the police tells him and what I tell him. Normally, there wouldn't have been any question, and it would automatically have been recorded as a death by misadventure."

"But, Malcolm, as you said, the actual cause of death wasn't really clear even to you, was it?"

"No, of course not, but in cases like this, sometimes we have to, well, simplify the findings a bit for the coroner. I'm sure he knows it, and it certainly makes his job easier. No, quine, personally I think that on this particular occasion somebody got to him. The coroner, I mean."

The image of the self-righteous Dr. Shah appeared instantly in Jean's mind when Anderson said that, but she simply thanked him for letting her know about the lab results. Slowly, she put down the phone and sat at her desk, thinking. If no poisons or drugs had been involved, that seemed to let several people off the hook—Anna McKenzie, Irene Kelso . . . But it looked as if there was something else—the word *diabolical* came unbidden to her mind—some other cause of death that neither she nor Douglas nor even Dr. Anderson had thought of. Jean knew, from her own experience, that the term "frightened to death" wasn't just a hyperbole. It could happen, particularly when the victim was already confused and weakened, as Kelso would have been after his operation. So it could still have been any one of them. Even Albert Caie.

Eleanor knocked on the door and came in. "You have a new patient," she said. "Thirty-nine years old and pregnant. No prenatal care. She thinks she's about to deliver."

Jean's brow furrowed. "I sometimes wonder why we bother with prenatal clinics," she said. "The ones who need them the most never show up." She sighed. "Have we ever seen her before? For anything else?"

"No. She's new in town. Came in from Dundee four weeks ago . . ." Eleanor hesitated, her eyes on Jean. "Actually, she's a widow," she said.

"Oh, poor thing," said Jean, her eyes full of compassion. "That's so sad. You remember that awful fire on the North Sea oil rig a few years ago? The wife of one of the men who died was in the hospital having her baby when it happened. For some reason I keep thinking about her."

"Yes, I remember that," said Eleanor. The disaster had filled the papers and TV news for days on end. "Shall I put her in the exam room?"

"Yes please. I'll be through in just a minute."

Mrs. Kitty Brewster was a quiet, plain-looking woman, with what looked like a permanently anxious expression on her face. She was pale, with gray, watery eyes, and the kind of frizzy brown hair that doesn't do well in a damp climate. To Jean's experienced eye, Kitty seemed about eight or nine months into her pregnancy. She was wearing a maternity skirt, and her ankles were both moderately swollen, which made Jean wonder about her blood pressure, which could sometimes become unstable in the latter stages of pregnancy.

Jean talked with her for a few moments, asked why she'd come to Perth, did she have friends in town, and so on. Jean always tried to have a little chat with new patients, not only to make them feel less scared about being in a doctor's examining room, but also to get a better idea of the person she was dealing with. One of Jean's most strongly held precepts was that the more she knew about a patient, the better she could take care of their ailments.

Kitty had worked as a teacher in a private school in Edinburgh, and had given up her job about three months before, when she'd started to show, and now she'd come to stay with her sister in Perth.

"Did you get any prenatal care in Edinburgh?" asked Jean.

Kitty looked away. "No," she said, "I didn't."

"Well, then," said Jean cheerfully. "We have a bit to catch up on. Now," she said, hoping that her question wouldn't start off a flood of tears, "can you tell me the approximate date of your conception?"

Kitty didn't burst into tears, but was obviously getting agitated, and Jean steeled herself to hear about the husband's death, presumably resulting from an accident or some other tragic event.

"My sister says you're a wonderful doctor," said Mrs. Brewster, making an effort to take hold of herself. "She said to tell you everything. And I haven't told *anybody* everything, not even her."

Jean took her hand and held it with womanly sympathy. It was sad how often a pregnancy could be a tragedy rather than a happy and joyous event, and Jean had a feeling that this was going to be one of the former kind. "Go ahead," she said.

"Well, I started having weird dreams, about, oh, ten months ago," said Kitty. Her voice was cultured, but low and hesitant. She watched Jean very carefully, and Jean knew that if a single hint of amusement or disbelief appeared on her face, Kitty Brewster would fall apart. So she fixed her expression into one of sympathetic attention, which was actually the way she was feeling.

"What kind of dreams?" asked Jean, who felt that there must have been some reason for Kitty to mention them.

"Does the word *incubus* mean anything to you?" asked Kitty.

"Isn't that a male spirit who comes and spends the night with a woman, then vanishes before daybreak?" asked Jean, smiling. "I always thought that was an intriguing idea—no socks to wash, no shirts to iron ..." Jean stopped abruptly, seeing Kitty's stricken look.

"Well, it was dreams like that I was having," said Kitty. "Except it was too real to be a dream. And it wasn't a spirit, it was ... a golden apparition. He would come in a blaze of light, full of love and majesty ... Dr. Montrose, he was something much *higher* than a spirit."

Jean sighed to herself. It was beginning to look as if Kitty were not quite mentally stable, or, as the girls said in their picturesque way, was out there where the buses don't run.

"You see," Kitty went on in a perfectly sanesounding voice, "my husband Walter died three and a half years ago with leukemia, and I haven't been with a man since then."

At that point Jean felt the hairs on the back of her neck rising, and she stared at Kitty. "You've never been with a man since then? Not even close?"

With complete certitude, Kitty shook her head. "No, not even close. I have, or had, many women friends," she said. "But I haven't even been to the cinema with a man."

"Is that why you left your job?" asked Jean.

"Yes. It would have been too embarrassing, because I didn't have a husband or a boyfriend, and I couldn't explain it rationally, or in terms that would be generally understandable." Kitty smiled, and Jean could feel something there, a kind of serenity about Kitty that was almost frightening. Jean went to church on Sundays, but wasn't particularly religious, and this was giving her goose bumps.

"I'd better examine you," she said.

"Yes, of course, Doctor," said Kitty, then added smilingly, "please be especially careful."

After checking her belly, which seemed about the right size for a full-term pregnancy, Jean took a fetal stethoscope and listened for about a minute, to pick up the baby's heartbeat. A strange expression crossed her face for a moment, then she positioned Kitty on the table with her feet in the stirrups, pulled on her latex gloves, and carried out a vaginal exam. She could feel the cervix, small, stiff, like the dimpled end of a little salami sausage. Jean pressed on it, gently moving the uterus. With her other hand she pressed very gently on Kitty's abdomen. After a few minutes, having completed a careful check of the other intrapelvic structures, Jean straightened up and pulled off her gloves. "I have some reassuring news for you, Kitty," she said, taking care not to show the mild amusement that she felt. "You're not pregnant. That mass in your tummy is most probably a very large fibroid, a benign tumor growing from the wall of the uterus, and of course it'll need to be removed."

Chapter 15

Douglas drove in through the Rose Street gate into the hospital grounds, up past the maternity wing and the rehab unit, to the main building. Finding a proper parking place was always difficult, but the lack of spaces didn't bother Doug for a moment. He left his car under a NO PARKING sign and, followed by Jamieson, walked in through the double doors, then to the elevator to the supervisor's office that Sandy Michie had allotted them. There was a note on a piece of pink paper attached to the telephone with a piece of paper tape, and Doug went over and picked it off the receiver. " 'Please phone Mr. Michie at extension 249,' " he read.

"I wonder what he wants," he muttered, scrunching up the paper and throwing it accurately into the wastebasket.

He picked up the phone, and while he dialed Mr. Michie's extension, said, "Jamieson, go and see if you can find Mrs. Doris Caie in the emergency room and bring her up here for a few minutes."

Jamieson nodded and went off.

Sandy Michie answered the phone himself, and he was not in a good mood. "I'm sorry, but you won't be able to use that office after tomorrow," he told Doug, his tone of voice stiff. "And another thing, if you still have to interview members of the hospital staff, I'd prefer that you do it outside their working hours."

"Ah, yes, Mr. Michie," said Douglas, who was in the mood for a fight. "Did you see the article in the paper? I thought you'd forbidden your staff to discuss this case with the press? Or do your employees routinely ignore your orders?"

Michie drew in his breath. "No, they do not, Inspector," he said, his voice furious. "And I will deal with *that* situation very quickly, I assure you."

"Well, I'm sure you know that people are already talking about a cover-up by the hospital authorities," went on Douglas in the same tone. "And if the word gets out that the administrator is going so far as to deny basic facilities to the police, and restricting their access to possible witnesses of a crime, it won't do the hospital's public image much good. Or your own, for that matter."

There was a silence. Doug could hear footsteps approaching down the corridor; Jamieson's clumping steps were unmistakable, and the lighter steps accompanying him were those of a woman, presumably Doris Caie.

"Very well," said Michie finally, in a tone that showed once again he had caved in. Doug's impression was that Michie was a man who went whichever way his loudest fears dictated. "I certainly want to give you all the assistance you require, in the hope that this matter can be quickly resolved. Can you tell me what progress you have made so far?"

The door opened, and Jamieson came in with Doris Caie, who looked scared out of her mind.

"Well, Mr. Michie, I think I can tell you that yes, we are making satisfactory progress," he said, staring hard at Doris Caie. "And I think we're about to make a whole lot more."

He put the phone down. The same predatory instinct that had made him go for Irene Kelso came once more to the surface, and he could feel the hunter's momentary quiver when about to make a kill.

"Well, Mrs. Caie," he said, "thank you for coming. Please sit down." He kept staring at her, in the way he knew intimidated people who were trying to keep information from him. If he'd ever looked that way at women outside the confines of his work, he would have run into instant trouble from husbands and boyfriends, but of course he never did.

"I'd like you to think back to last Saturday evening," he said, "when Robertson Kelso was admitted."

Doris Caie drew in her breath and looked at Douglas, obviously making a big effort to pull herself together. Her eyes were big, pale, and a little bulging. Jamieson, watching, thought she looked as if she'd been hypnotized.

"Did you leave the emergency room at any time during your shift?" asked Doug, starting off gently.

Doris kept looking back at Douglas with an expression that was beginning to unnerve him. "No. Unless you count going to the bathroom. They don't have one in Emergency, and the nearest one's halfway down the main corridor."

"Did you have any visitors while you were at work?" If Douglas meant to scare her with his tone of voice, it was hard to tell whether he'd succeeded.

"No, I didn't," she answered. Douglas took a big breath, but she went on before he could say anything, "my *husband* did come to pick me up, but that was a few minutes after the shift was over. And I'm not sure he would come under the heading of *visitor*."

Doug exhaled slowly. This woman might be more of a challenge than he'd originally expected. And she had the look, that he quickly recognized, of a person who had thought hard, and had carefully prepared what she was going to say. Also she seemed to have got over her initial fear of being interrogated by the police.

"So he came to pick you up, did he? Which implies that he had taken you to the hospital at the start of your shift, doesn't it? Your husband runs a little taxi service, just for you? That's really nice."

Doris said nothing. Douglas waited, until it was clear that she considered his questions rhetorical and wasn't going to answer them.

"Okay, Mrs. Caie," he said, his tone hardening. Sometimes Douglas had dreams of being an interrogator in the old Lubyanka prison under the Soviet regime. At least he wouldn't have had to worry about civil rights or any of that nonsense, and eventually they always got the correct answers. "Did your husband bring you to the hospital when you went to work that day?"

"Albert? No, he didn't. He was at work. I have my own car, and I drive myself to the hospital."

"Then, Mrs. Caie," said Douglas, trying to keep the triumph out of his voice, "how was it that if you had driven yourself to the hospital and your car was presumably there waiting in the parking area, that you needed to be picked up?"

"It wasn't working properly," replied Doris quickly. "It died just as I was parking it when I came to work. So I called Albert later, and he said he'd come and pick me up when my shift was over."

"So your husband drove you home," said Douglas in a voice that expressed little more than boredom.

"No. He fixed my car. It was just one of the battery terminals that had got loose, he said."

Douglas sat up a little straighter. "So you both went home in different cars, and met up at home, right?"

Doris made no sign of agreement or disagreement, and Douglas was beginning to see that this woman was intelligent, and if he wanted to avoid embarrassment, he would have to be a bit more precise and stop asking leading questions.

He was formulating his next question when Doris answered it. "Albert didn't come home immediately," she said. "On Saturdays he often goes off to the pub by himself."

"And at what time did he get home?"

"I don't know," Doris replied. "I was tired, and went to bed and fell asleep immediately. I didn't hear him come in."

"Mrs. Caie, your husband was seen loitering on the hospital premises late that night, on the fourth floor, where Robertson Kelso was found dead later on that morning."

Again, Doris said nothing, and her expression didn't change.

"And as it is well-known that Mr. Caie and Mr. Kelso were bitter enemies, the suggestion has been made that Mr. Caie may have had something to do with Kelso's death."

"I don't know anything about that," said Doris. She looked Douglas straight in the eye. "It seems to me that Albert is the one you should be talking to."

"We'll get to him in due course, I assure you," said Douglas in his most ponderous voice. "Meanwhile, I'd like to ask you if you have any other thoughts about this sad matter."

A very small, thin smile appeared on Doris's face. "Sad?" she said. "You're the only person in the city of Perth who thinks so. Everybody else who knew Robertson Kelso is very happy that he's dead. *And that includes me.*" Doris said the last four words with a curious emphasis. "And now," she said, standing up, "if that's all, Inspector, I have to get back to work. We're shorthanded today down in Emergency, and I can't be away too long."

"It isn't quite all," said Douglas. "Do you know if your husband possesses any kind of firearm?"

"A gun?" Doris thought for a moment. It seemed to Douglas that she was not searching in her mind for the truth, but rather for some answer that would satisfy him without perjuring herself. "Not that I know of," she said carefully, then, "Was Kelso shot?"

"No," replied Doug, feeling annoyed. "He wasn't shot. I'm sure you know that the cause of death was undetermined."

"Then, what does it matter if Albert owns a gun or not?"

"Because carrying a deadly weapon is a felony, and so is threatening the life of another individual," said Doug grimly. "And we have information that leads us to believe that both of these occurred."

"Well, there seems to be a lot of loose talk going on about this case," said Doris, her words more emphatic than her tone, which remained meek and a little scared. "But so far there seems to be very little that can be proven. I'm quite sure that Albert can satisfactorily answer any questions you may have for him. Now, if you'll excuse me, I really must get back downstairs."

After Mrs. Caie had gone, Doug and Jamieson looked at each other rather blankly for a few moments, then Doug sent Jamieson off to find Anna McKenzie, but she was in the middle of a case and wouldn't be finished for at least two hours.

When he came back, Doug sat him down and they went over the various possibilities. Douglas wasn't particularly interested in Jamieson's thoughts on the subject; he made use of him in the way a tennis player might practice his strokes by hitting the ball against a blank wall.

"Two basic possibilities exist here, Jamieson," he said, putting up two fingers. "One is that Kelso's death was unavoidable, accidental, and not anybody's fault. Are you listening to me?" His voice went up a little, irritated at Jamieson's apparent lack of attention.

"Yes, sir," replied Jamieson, bringing his gaze down from the ceiling. "You said that two basic possibilities exist."

"Right. The other is that it was done on purpose, by a person or persons unknown. In other words, that Robertson Kelso was murdered."

"Actually, sir, that's the only possibility."

Douglas had already drawn breath for his exposition on the second possibility, and raised his eyebrows irritably. "And how did you arrive at that conclusion, Jamieson?"

"Not me, sir. It was the coroner who said so."

"Well, yes, that's true ..." Douglas shrugged,

as if the coroner's opinion was a matter of minor importance. "But as police officers we have to take the first possibility into consideration." Doug put his hands flat on the desk. "Which brings us to possible motives for killing the man."

"Mr. Kirkwall has the strongest one," said Jamieson promptly. "Kelso stole his wife."

"Certainly, a point to consider," said Doug heavily. "But we mustn't come to hasty conclusions. There are plenty of others who could have done it."

"You asked for motives," said Jamieson, sounding sulky. "I just gave you one."

"Right. Other motives in this case might include revenge. I'm thinking of Albert Caie in particular. Which could include Mrs. Caie, but I don't really think so."

"Aye, and we still haven't talked to him," said Jamieson.

"We'll go and see him when we leave here," said Douglas. He stared thoughtfully across the desk at Jamieson. "And then, of course, we have our wily Oriental friend, Dr. Ramashandra Shah."

"He's Indian, sir. That makes him Asian, not Oriental."

"Whatever. He's not Scottish, we know that, so where he actually came from doesn't really matter. We do know that he's a treacherous, underhanded fellow, just what you'd expect from a foreigner, especially an *Oriental* foreigner. We know he's one of the few people who hates Mr. Kirkwall, and he had plenty of occasion to get at Kelso, and when he died it was a good opportunity to put the blame on Mr. Kirkwall, which he very promptly did."

"Because Mr. Kirkwall was in his way professionally?" Jamieson looked puzzled. "You said that once before, but I didn't understand why. They're both doctors, in different fields, so I don't see why they would get in each other's way."

"Professional jealousy," replied Douglas, nodding as if the serpentine inner politics of the hospital were an open book to him. "Mr. Kirkwall was very highly thought of before he started drinking, and he was up there in the hierarchy at the hospital. For years, he's been in charge of the important decision-making committees, and Shah wants to take over from him."

"He wants it bad enough to kill somebody?"

"With foreigners you never know," said Douglas, nodding gravely. "And the Oriental mind is a riddle inside a mystery."

"Wrapped in an enigma," added Jamieson, who had been reading an illustrated life of Winston Churchill.

Douglas stared at Jamieson. They'd worked together for some years now, but sometimes Douglas felt he didn't know anything at all about his subordinate.

"How about Dr. McKenzie, sir?" asked Jamieson. "Would you consider her a suspect?"

"Everyone's a suspect," said Douglas sententiously. "As for her, I think she has the hots for Mr. Kirkwall. She could have knocked off Kelso because of what he'd done to Mr. Kirkwall. She could have done it with any one of those powerful drugs those anesthetists use. And the tests can't always identify them."

Jamieson thought about that.

Doug glanced at his notepad. "Next, there's the supervisor, Mrs. . . ."

"Gallacher," said Jamieson. "Rosemary Gallacher."

"Right. She was on duty all the time that Kelso was in the hospital. But nobody's ever suggested that she had anything against Kelso or Mr. Kirkwall, for that matter. She seems a nice, competent woman who was just doing her job that night. Was that your impression?"

Jamieson hesitated. "I don't know," he said. "When we were talking to her, she seemed very controlled, but underneath she was scared. I thought so, anyway."

That had not been Douglas's recollection of their interview, held the day after he'd spoken unofficially to her at Jean Montrose's house. "Scared of what?" he asked.

"I don't know. But her voice was shaking, and she had her hands in her lap, and they were clasped so tightly her knuckles were white. You must have seen that."

Douglas repressed a shrug of annoyance. It seemed that whenever Jamieson was asked for his opinion on anything, he took on a patronizing tone that infuriated Douglas.

"I canna say that I did," he said. When provoked, Douglas's Glasgow accent became more pronounced. "Anyway, a lot of people get nervous talking to us. They don't have to be guilty of anything."

"Like Mrs. Kelso?"

Douglas stood up and looked out of the window. Down below, the interminable string of lorries and cars going slowly around the traffic circle simply increased his sense of frustration and futility. He turned around. "Damn it, Jamieson!" he exploded. "I really hate this kind of case. We don't even know for sure that a crime's been committed, but here we are, forced to spend our valuable time investigating." He smacked his hand on a pile of papers at the side of his desk. "As if there wasn't plenty of other work that needs to be done."

"We were going to talk to Mr. Caie, sir," said Jamieson after a pause.

"Right," replied Douglas. He pointed to the telephone. "Make sure he's at home."

After Albert's business had been destroyed by Robertson Kelso, the Caies had moved into a small flat on the Bridgend side of the river, in a multistory building that used to belong to the city and had been sold, mostly to the tenants, during the Thatcher era. There was a small sign on the lift informing them that it was temporarily out of service, adding that the repair company apologized for any inconvenience it had caused. So, grumbling, Douglas and Jamieson had to trudge up to the sixth floor.

"You're not in the best of shape, Jamieson," said

Douglas, leaning on the metal banister at the fifth floor. "You're wheezing."

"It's my allergies, sir," replied Jamieson, snuffling. "They're always bad at this time of year."

Albert Caie was at home, unshaven and aggressive-looking when he opened the door.

"So somebody saw me, huh," he said in an unpleasant voice, after Doug and Jamieson had come into the flat and told him the reason for their visit. "And that same somebody reported me? Well, it's my word against theirs, isn't it?" Both Albert's scowling face and rasping voice gave an impression of perpetual anger, without any alleviating humor.

"*Two* people said they saw you," said Douglas patiently, "so don't waste our time denying it."

"Well, it isn't a crime, is it?"

"What isn't a crime, Mr. Caie?" asked Douglas, still gentle, but Jamieson could detect traces of the chill that usually preceded Doug's hammer blows.

"Hanging around the hospital after hours."

"Was Mr. Kelso awake when you came into his room?"

"I didn't say I came into his room."

Doug stood up, swiftly and threateningly enough to make Caie jump. "Mr. Caie," he said, "you have a choice. Either cooperate or you come down to the station with us. In handcuffs, and with as much publicity as we can drum up." Doug looked at his watch. "I don't want to put undue pressure on you," he said. "I'll give you five seconds to decide."

"Okay," replied Caie. "I've got nothing to hide. Actually, I don't even care now. I'm just glad he's dead, that bastard."

"You own a gun, Mr. Caie?"

Some of the furrows in Albert's face deepened momentarily. "Not now. I did, though. I've thrown it away."

"Where?"

"I don't remember. Anyway, Kelso wasn't shot, so why do you care?"

"Did you have a licence for that gun?"

"No."

"Do you know that possession of an unlicenced gun is a felony punishable by a heavy fine plus a prison sentence?"

Caie shrugged, as if he simply didn't care anymore, and Douglas watched him with interest, knowing that people with that attitude could be more dangerous than anyone, because they had no fear of punishment. Doug felt pretty sure that if Caie *had* pulled the trigger on Kelso, he'd have quietly given himself up and admitted what he'd done.

"Did you inject any drug or other substance into Mr. Kelso while you were in his room?"

"No. You can ask Irene, his wife. She was there, she'll tell you, if she hasn't already."

"While you were at the hospital, did you see anyone or anything suspicious?" As soon as he'd spoken the words, Douglas realized how silly they sounded, and his face went slightly pink.

Caie stared at him. "Yes, as a matter of fact, I

did," he said. "In the fourth floor men's toilet, at about one-thirty."

Douglas's jaw dropped for a moment. This was a totally unexpected development, and he sat up very straight in his chair. "All right, then, Mr. Caie, who or what did you see there that aroused your suspicions?"

"My reflection in the mirror," answered Caie.

Douglas and Jamieson left soon after.

"I feel sorry for Caie," said Jamieson as they drove back across the old Tay bridge. "He lost everything because of Kelso, his money, his business, his reputation. His life's over. I still think he had the most powerful motive to kill Kelso."

Chapter 16

Jean usually went up to the hospital once or twice a week, to keep an eye on her patients who had been admitted there. She worked hard to keep her patients out of the hospital, but of course situations occasionally arose where home care was no longer adequate for her unstable diabetics, or older people with pneumonia, and surgical problems at any age.

Today Jean was on her way to visit Kitty Brewster when she met Dr. Peter MacIntosh, the head of obstetrics and gynecology, who had operated on Kitty that morning. He and Jean had known each other professionally for many years, and were good friends.

"I was going to phone you later, Jean," he said, stopping in the corridor. Peter was tall, good-looking, with prematurely white hair and a lanky, relaxed ease about him. "Your patient Mrs. Brewster, did very well after her operation," he said. "That was one huge fibroid we took out of her. It weighed over ten pounds." He put both hands out in front of him as if he were holding a melon, to give Jean an idea of the size of the tumor.

"Still, that was less trouble than the alternative might have been," said Jean, smiling. She told him about Kitty's dreams. "Kitty was pretty well convinced that she was going to be a major participant in the Second Coming," she said. "And for a wee while she almost had me convinced, too."

They walked along the corridor together, an unlikely pair. Peter was a slim six foot two, and Jean was not so slim and a shade over five feet. Suddenly, Peter stopped and looked down worriedly at Jean. "A lot of us are really concerned about Hugh Kirkwall," he said. "And a couple of days ago he told me that he'd talked to you about his problems with Shah."

"Did something new happen?" asked Jean, concerned.

"Well, Shah seems to be stepping up his campaign," said Peter. "Now he's been contacting individual hospital board members and trying to convince them to convene a special meeting to get rid of Hugh." Peter flushed with embarrassment and annoyance at the actions of his troublesome colleague. "Shah's really turning this hospital upside down," he went on. "I've never met anybody so . . . so relentlessly ambitious."

"What do you think will happen?" asked Jean.

Peter sighed. "Unless someone can find out what actually happened to Robertson Kelso, how he died, it doesn't look good," he said. "It's really a shame, because Hugh's completely stopped drinking, and as you know he's a very competent surgeon, and very good at running his commit- tees." Peter's usually cheerful gaze clouded. "Shah's competent enough, I suppose, but he wouldn't be a patch on Hugh if he did replace him. There's always strife and dissension when Shah's around." Peter glanced around to make sure they were alone, before going on. "Jean, do you think that Shah could have had anything to do with Kelso's death?"

"Peter, to me the biggest problem is still *how* he died," said Jean. "And that is still a mystery. Malcolm Anderson's still trying to figure it out, but at this point he just doesn't know. He can't tell whether he died accidentally or not. And until we do know, I don't see any way to figure out *who*, if anyone, did it."

A door opened at the far end of the corridor, and behind Peter's tall figure Jean saw a slim, white-coated figure starting to walk toward them. She was too far for Jean to be certain, but it looked like Anna McKenzie, the anesthesiologist. Jean turned her attention back to Peter. "And until we do know," she went on, "I don't see any end to all these accusations, insinuations, and behind-the- scenes plotting, do you, Peter?"

"Well, it's bad for the hospital," said Peter un- happily. "Everybody's starting to take sides, and all that press and TV coverage is giving our pa- tients a terrible impression about this place."

"The police are investigating," said Jean, but there wasn't much hope in her voice. "Maybe they'll come up with something that will explain it all."

Anna McKenzie came up to them. "Oh, Jean," she exclaimed. "I'm glad you're here. I was going to phone you . . . Do you have a minute?"

"I'll talk to you later, Jean," said Peter, moving off.

Anna waited a moment for Peter to get out of earshot, then her face seemed to change. Her lower lip quivered. "Jean, I know that Hugh spoke to you . . . I'm very worried about him. He's getting very withdrawn, he's avoiding his friends, and he's not talking to anyone. He's stopped drinking, but he's so angry and upset with all that's been going on, that . . ." Anna paused, her big blue eyes fixed on Jean's. "Well, I'm afraid something terrible might happen to him."

"Anna," asked Jean quietly, "are you *involved* with him?"

"I wish," replied Anna frankly. "I like him a lot . . . a whole lot. But I don't think he really knows that I exist. I mean as a *person*. He's nice to me, of course," she went on quickly, "but then he's nice to everybody." She laughed, a brittle, transparent laugh, through which the pain was apparent. "Except of course to that horrible Dr. Shah . . ." Anna's lips tightened. "I really hate that man. He's making life impossible for Hugh, and the sad thing is that there isn't much Hugh can do about it."

"I'm sure Hugh has a lot of support," said Jean. "Everybody knows how competent he is, and everybody likes him. I'm sure he'll be able to weather this storm. He's weathered others."

"Well, yes, I suppose so . . ." Anna hesitated. "But a lot of people are upset about all this, and some of them feel that to some extent, Hugh's to blame. And I suppose that's true. But the result is that now just about everybody's sitting on the sidelines, waiting to see what happens."

"We're all waiting to see what happens, Anna," said Jean, watching her. "I just wish we had a few more answers, or at least a few hints about what happened to Robertson Kelso."

Anna's pager went off, a quiet beep from her pocket. "I have to run," she said. "Nice talking to you, Jean." She hesitated for a moment. "I hope something happens soon to get Hugh off the hook. It's driving me out of my mind . . ." Bright tears suddenly appeared in her eyes, and she turned quickly and walked back toward the operating theatre.

Kitty Brewster, now back in her own room after a stay in the recovery area, was suffering some postoperative pain, and seemed pleased to see Jean. But there was something, a kind of dissatisfaction in her voice when she answered Jean's question about being pleased with the outcome.

"Yes, I suppose so," she said, very seriously, looking under the sheets at her abdomen, now flat, under the surgical dressing. "I'll be able to go back to work, and all that, which is certainly a big relief." She gave Jean a quaint, rather sad look, as if she wasn't sure she should say anything. "I just wonder why God decided to change his mind."

Chapter 17

"Inspector Niven?"

It was five in the evening, and Douglas was getting ready to go home. He recognized Dr. Shah's voice, and felt a combination of annoyance and mistrust at his well-remembered high, insistent tone.

"Yes?"

"This is Dr. Ramashandra Shah, Inspector, and I have some further information about the death of Mr. Robertson Kelso," said Shah in a tone full of self-satisfaction. "This information will prove to you beyond any doubt that the patient's death was not accidental, and which will also establish the guilt of the individual involved."

Douglas reached for a pen. "Go ahead, Doctor," he said. "I'm listening."

"I don't believe I should divulge this information over the telephone, Inspector," said Shah with his infuriating smoothness. "I would like to tell you in person before I make this information available to the press."

"The press? *You*'re going to tell the press? Have you checked this with Mr. Michie?"

"I haven't been able to reach Mr. Michie," replied Shah. "I understand that he's away at a conference in Dundee. So, as this matter is of great importance to the public, I have had to make my own decision about it."

Douglas shrugged. "Where are you now?"

"In the emergency room at the hospital. I'll be taking a break in about three hours, at eight o'clock. Could you meet me in the doctors' lounge at the hospital? There's never anyone there at that time."

"Where is that? The lounge?"

"On the third floor. You get out of the lift, sir, and turn left. It's the last door at the end of the corridor on the right. The door is marked PRIVATE."

"Eight o'clock, then, Doctor."

"Yes, sir, thank you."

Douglas put the phone down and sighed. He felt sure that Shah didn't have anything real to add, and was just bent on making more trouble for Mr. Kirkwall, but he couldn't ignore his request. He made a notation on his desk calendar, called Jamieson to tell him to meet him at the hospital at eight, put some papers in his old briefcase, and headed for home.

Cathie heard his car stop outside the house and opened the door for him. Still pretty, she wore a bright apron over her faded print dress, and a scarf protected her curly brown hair from kitchen smells. She was carrying Douglas, Jr. balanced on her hip. He was half asleep, but smiled when he saw his daddy beaming at him over his mother's shoulder.

"He had his whooping cough shot today," she informed Douglas after giving him a big kiss. "He didn't like it much, although Dr. Montrose gave him the injection herself."

"Did you cry?" Douglas gave his son a playfully fierce look.

"Not much," said Cathie. She bounced Douglas, Jr. gently on her hip. "You didn't, did you, my wee beauty?"

"Do you think he remembers her?" asked Douglas, his expression suddenly becoming very serious.

"From when he was born? I dinna think he would, do you?" She stroked her son's head, while they both thought about how they had almost lost him, and how Jean Montrose had just managed to resuscitate him. Cathie shivered. "I pray for her every night, you know."

"Me, too," agreed Douglas, then added with his customary honesty. "When I remember."

"I'm going to put him upstairs in his cot," said Cathie, and went up the narrow stairs to the bedroom.

"What's for dinner?" Douglas called up after her. "Whatever it is, it smells good."

"Mince and tatties," she said, looking back over her shoulder. "Your favorite. And then apple crumble."

"It must be Thursday," he said, but she was already upstairs and didn't hear him. Douglas could faintly hear her voice, talking gentle baby talk to their son. He took a bottle of Watneys out of the fridge, opened it, and took it through to the living room, where he unfolded the newspaper and started to read, thinking what a lucky, contented, and happy person he was.

When Cathie came down again she was without apron or scarf, and they sat in companionable silence while their dinner simmered in the kitchen.

"How's your case going?" asked Cathie after they sat down at the table and she was filling his plate.

"Och, you know, nothing great," he replied. "I don't know why I get all the weird problems around this town."

"It's because you're the only one who can solve them," said Cathie proudly. "Is that enough peas for you? There's plenty more." She put the pan back on the stove with the gas turned as low as it would go. "I was in Strathdee's this afternoon getting butteries for tomorrow's breakfast," she went on, "and there was this woman in front of me saying that they'd never find out who killed Robertson Kelso. 'Don't be so sure,' I told her. 'Why, what do you know about it?' she says to me, turning around, and so I said to her, smiling, like, 'that's for me to know and you to guess,' and then Yvette, the girl who was serving, told her."

"Told her what?" In spite of certain prejudices he had about listening to women's gossip, Douglas enjoyed hearing about Cathie's encounters in the real world, and it made him feel that he was participating in the general life of the town, however indirectly.

"Yvette told her who I was, and more to the point, who *you* were. That settled the woman's hash, I can tell you that." Cathie served herself, smiling happily, delighted to have basked in her husband's reflected glory.

"She was probably right, though," said Doug gloomily through a mouthful of mince and mashed potatoes. "We may never find out who did it. Is there any more gravy?"

"It's right in front of you," replied Cathie. "While the bairn was getting his shot, I was talking to Dr. Montrose. You know how everybody's talking about the Kelso business, saying it was Mr. Kirkwall's fault. If he didn't do it on purpose, they're saying, it was because he wasna in full command of his ... What's that expression, Doug?"

"Drunk," replied Douglas.

"Yes, well, when I mentioned that to Dr. Montrose, she said that she was *certain* that wasn't true."

"She doesn't always know everything about a case, you know. And certainly not about this one." Although Douglas had the greatest respect for Jean's opinion, he thought that Cathie's regard for her verged on idolatry, and that gave him occasional slight twinges of jealousy.

Cathie was about to make a retort when they heard first a whimper, then a yell from upstairs.

"He's got your lungs, all right," said Cathie. She

put her napkin on the table and went upstairs, to reappear a few moments later with Douglas, Jr. "He's hungry," she explained. "The injection put him off his supper."

Cathie put some peas in a saucer and started to mash them with her fork. She sat down with Douglas, Jr. on her lap and started to feed him. He coughed on the third mouthful, and sprayed pale green fragments over the tablecloth.

"Lucky it's the same green as the tablecloth," said Douglas, starting to wipe up with his napkin.

"Just leave it." Cathie got up and fetched a wet rag from the kitchen and scrubbed vigorously at the spots.

"I have to go up to the hospital," said Douglas, looking at the clock. "That Dr. Shah," he went on with heavy humor, "I think he's going to confess to everything tonight."

"Take care," said Cathie, looking worried. "I never like you going out to work after dinner."

"You always say that," said Douglas, smiling. He kissed her on the forehead. "I've been going out in the evenings for years, and nothing's ever happened. Well, nothing really serious."

Ten minutes later, Douglas pulled up outside the hospital's main entrance. He could see Jamieson waiting for him near the door, his bulky figure silhouetted in front of the lights in the lobby.

Together they walked along the main corridor on the ground floor until they came to the lift. Douglas pressed the button, and they waited in silence. Douglas felt unaccountably tense; he didn't like the hospital, and he didn't like Dr. Shah, but there was something else there that was making him feel as if he might jump out of his skin.

The third floor was deserted, and their feet clattered on the hard, shiny floor all the way to the end. They stopped in front of the door marked PRIVATE.

"This must be it," said Douglas. He knocked lightly and went in, holding the door for Jamieson.

There were only a few dim lights on in the room. Dr. Shah was sitting in a deep leather easy chair at the far end of the room. Some papers lay open on the low table in front of him.

"Good evening, Dr. Shah," said Douglas, coming up. Then he saw that Dr. Shah's head was at a curious angle, and he was very still. Coming closer, they saw that his tongue was protruding, and that he was quite dead, but it took Douglas a minute before he noticed the thin, deep red-blue marks around Shah's neck, and realized that he had been garroted.

"He's still warm," said Jamieson.

Chapter 18

"Well, there's no doubt about the cause of death in this one," said Dr. Anderson, looking around at Douglas and Jamieson. Dr. Shah's naked body, lying on the stainless-steel autopsy table, looked slimmer and more fragile-looking in death than he had in life. "This was done with a loop of wire, maybe a piece of piano wire, with a handle at each end."

"Isn't that how the French Resistance people used to kill German sentries?" asked Jamieson.

"Yes." Malcolm Anderson had an encyclopedic knowledge of the cruelties that men had practiced on each other over the centuries, and he liked to display his erudition. "The garrote was originally a carter's stick," he informed Doug and Jamieson, "and highwaymen would strangle their victims with it." He demonstrated how that was done, from behind, holding the stick in the crook of their elbows and pushing the victim's head forward over it with their hands. "Since then," he went on, "the technique has evolved and changed. For instance, in Spain the garrote was a metal collar attached to a post, and a screw was turned slowly to strangle the victim. There's a pen-and-ink sketch by Goya that shows the technique rather well. Did you know that the Spaniards were still executing prisoners that way right up into the 1960s?"

"How barbaric," murmured Doug. "But what else would you expect from a gang of foreigners? It certainly isn't a natural, decent, Scottish way of killing anybody," he went on, looking at Shah's partially dissected neck with some distaste. "Although, I must say, it's less messy than most."

"It looks as if the perpetrator was trying to cut his head off," said Jamieson. Indeed the wire had cut through the skin and soft tissues of the neck.

"Death is caused by a combination of asphyxia and shutting off the blood supply to the brain," said Dr. Anderson, now well into his lecturing mode, "and it is usually rapid. In medieval times, prisoners condemned to be burned at the stake could often pay the executioner to strangle them first, as it was considered an almost painless way to die. A certain Major Richardson, observing such executions in Spain, said it was the most manly and visually the least offensive method he'd come across . . ." As he talked, Anderson was dissecting the larynx. "See the hemorrhage, here?" he asked, pointing at the compressed windpipe. "This garroting was done with a lot of force."

"Could a woman do this?" asked Douglas.

"Yes, I suppose so, but it's generally a male method of execution. It's not that it requires a great deal of force, as the main element is surprise, but you have to know how to do it. The military get taught how to do it in unarmed combat schools, so you might want to look in that direction first."

Doug and Jamieson glanced at each other. Soon after their discovery of Shah's body, they had left the situation in the hands of the photographer and the forensic unit, and had gone to Hugh Kirkwall's home, where he was watching the TV. Douglas cautioned him in the usual way, and Hugh listened, apparently astonished. Yes, he told them, after Douglas's brief recitation was over, he had been up at the hospital earlier in the evening, seeing patients he'd operated on earlier in the day.

"And what time was this, Doctor?"

"Well, I came in after dinner, maybe six-thirty."

"And at what time did you leave?"

"I was there about an hour. Actually, I left the hospital just before twenty minutes to eight. Now, would you like to tell me why you're asking?"

"How are you so sure of the time?" asked Doug.

"I looked at the clock."

"Which clock?" persisted Douglas.

"The one in the doctors' lounge,"

"Was there anyone else there? In the lounge?"

"No. There's never anybody there at that time . . ." But a strange look had passed over Hugh's face. When he saw that Douglas was watching him, he said, "Actually, someone was coming in just as I was leaving through the end door. There are two doors," he explained unnecessarily. "One at each end of the room."

"Did you see who it was, coming in?"

"I'm not certain, but I think it was Dr. Shah." A look of anger passed momentarily over his face. "I didn't stop to make sure."

"Try to remember, Mr. Kirkwall," urged Douglas.

"I'm not saying another word until you tell me what this is about," said Mr. Kirkwall firmly.

Douglas thought for a moment. "All right, then," he said, watching Mr. Kirkwall narrowly. "One of your colleagues was found dead at the hospital this evening. He had earlier told us he had some vital information to give us concerning Robertson Kelso's death."

"It wasn't Dr. Shah, by any chance?" Hugh was watching Douglas just as carefully, and a slow smile spread over his face. "How terribly sad."

"I didn't say it was Dr. Shah," said Douglas coolly. "And I'd be most interested to hear why you thought he might be the victim."

"I suppose he just came to my mind. Or maybe it was just wishful thinking on my part. Anyway, just because he's dead . . ." Hugh stopped, and his eyes widened slightly. "Oh, now, wait a minute. You said 'victim.' Are you telling me that his death was not natural?"

"Were you ever in the military, sir?" asked Douglas.

"No. Why? Did somebody drive a tank over him? I'd have really enjoyed seeing that."

"No, sir. Dr. Shah was actually asphyxiated."

"Strangled?" Kirkwall's expression became somber. "Oh, dear. Look, I'm sorry if I sounded frivolous a minute ago. You know that Shah was no friend of mine, but I wouldn't do him any physical harm. Not that I hadn't thought about it . . ." Hugh grinned in a lopsided, embarrassed way.

"I'd like an exact account of your movements this evening, please, sir. And the names of the people who can corroborate your statements."

"Let's see . . . I was at the hospital all afternoon. I dictated some reports about four-thirty, finished them around five, and went home."

"Can anyone confirm that, sir?"

Hugh thought. "Shala Green, who's in charge of records, she was there. I asked her for a fresh tape."

"Would you spell that name, please, sir?" asked Jamieson, and Hugh did so.

"Did anyone see you leave the hospital?" Doug's voice was controlled, not quite aggressive.

"I went through the emergency room, but I don't know if anyone saw me."

"And what time was that, sir?"

"Just a little after five."

"And you came home."

"Yes. I had dinner, then went back about six-thirty."

"Did anyone see you come in?"

I stopped at the desk in the emergency room, and talked with the nurse on duty. Then I saw the evening supervisor, Mrs. Gallacher, in the corridor and talked to her for a minute about one of my patients. After that I did my rounds . . ." Hugh took a black leather-bound notebook out of his pocket and opened it. "These are the patients I visited, with their room numbers."

Douglas glanced at the list of five patients.

"And then?"

"Then I went over to the operating theatre to check times for tomorrow."

"What time was that?"

"Let's see . . . that must have been about seven-thirty."

"Did you talk to anyone there?"

"Dr. McKenzie. She was on call." A very faint flush appeared on Hugh's face, and Douglas was on to it instantly.

"And what might you have talked about, you and Dr. McKenzie?"

Douglas shifted in his chair and didn't answer for a moment. "Dr. McKenzie's a bit overwrought at the present time," he said finally. "I'm sure you know that she's very upset about the business with Robertson Kelso."

"Yes, we are aware of that, Mr. Kirkwall," replied Douglas in his heavy voice.

"Well, Anna was warning me about Dr. Shah. According to her, he was going to send a letter to the Tay Health Board stating the facts of the Kelso case as he saw them and asking them to remove me from my job here. Apparently, Dr. Shah was going to send a copy to the *Courier* and the TV stations, Grampian and the BBC. Poor Anna, she was a lot more upset than I was."

"Did you talk about anything else?"

Hugh hesitated for a moment. "No," he said.

"You don't seem quite sure of your reply, Mr. Kirkwall," said Douglas grimly. "So I'll repeat my question. Did you and Dr. McKenzie talk about any other matter whatsoever?"

"She asked if I'd like to come and have dinner with her sometime later in the week."

Douglas nodded. "And what did you reply?"

"I thanked her, said it was very nice of her to think of it, but I wasn't feeling very sociable these days, so I turned her invitation down."

"How did she handle that?"

"Well, as I said, she was already upset . . . she cried, and held on to my arm . . ."

"Where exactly did this occur, Mr. Kirkwall?"

"There's a little corridor in the operating suite, with the changing rooms on either side. In that corridor."

"Was there anyone else there?"

"No. I think there was a nurse somewhere in the suite. The lights were on, and I heard someone moving around, but I didn't see anyone."

"And then?"

"I went home."

"Did you stop off anywhere on the way?"

"The doctors' lounge, as I told you. Mostly to check for messages. Each doctor has a box there for local mail and messages."

"Did you have any mail?"

"A couple of pieces. Lab reports, announcements of committee meetings, that kind of thing."

"Did you read them there or take them home?"

"I read them there."

"And what time was that?"

"About twenty minutes to eight."

"Did anyone else come in while you were in the lounge?"

"No. As I told you, someone was coming in as I was leaving. I thought it might be Shah, but I couldn't swear to it."

"What was this person wearing?"

"I've no idea. I just saw the door open and had only the slightest glimpse of the person."

"Tall, short?"

Kirkwall shook his head. "I don't know."

"A man? A woman?"

The phone on the table by the door rang, startlingly loud. Hugh picked it up, then held it out to Doug. "It's for you."

Dr. Malcolm Anderson was at the other end. "I don't think our friend here could have been dead for more than a few minutes when you found him," he said. "His body temperature was almost normal, and the room isn't that warm."

Doug thanked him, then asked to speak to Bev Price, the leader of the forensic team. "Did you find any fingerprints?" he asked her.

"Yes. Lots. On the door handles, the chair arms, tables, everywhere. Dozens of them, but most of them too smeared to use."

"Anything else?"

"Not so far. We're vacuuming for hairs and fibers, but so many people use this place I don't know how useful it's going to be."

"The weapon?" As he spoke, Douglas turned a quick eye on Mr. Kirkwall.

"Nothing." He put the phone down slowly.

"I thought you said he'd been strangled," said Kirkwall, after Doug had sat down again. "Then you asked them about a weapon?"

"Strangulation doesn't necessarily mean *manual* strangulation, as I'm sure you're well aware, Mr. Kirkwall. And in this case it wasn't. Anyway, you were telling us about the person you saw come into the lounge as you were leaving."

"I've told you." Kirkwall thought for a moment. "Actually," he went on, "the person seemed to hesitate for a second and then backed out, as if he or she didn't want to be seen."

"Mr. Kirkwall, can you think of anyone who might have enough reason to kill Dr. Shah?"

"You mean anyone besides me? No, I don't think so. Dr. Shah was generally disliked, I think, but unless he had other enemies outside the hospital, I can't think of anybody."

Very deliberately, Douglas stood up, as did Jamieson a moment after him.

"Mr. Kirkwall," said Douglas in his most formal tone, "we will probably need you to come down to headquarters to make a formal statement within the next twenty-four hours concerning the murder of Dr. Ramashandra Shah. Until then, you are not to leave Perth without specific permission from me. Is that clear?"

Kirkwall nodded, looking as if he couldn't quite believe what he was hearing. As they left, Jamieson fixed Hugh with a scowl that suggested he would personally deal with him if he was unwise enough to stray beyond the city limits.

"So what do you think?" asked Douglas as they drove back to the hospital.

"He did it," said Jamieson, "no question."

Chapter 19

Jean didn't hear about Shah's death until the next morning. She had got up quietly, wakened both girls, and was making breakfast when she turned on the radio; it was the first item on the local news. Jean sat down on the stool as if she'd been slapped in the face. "Dear God," she thought, "what is happening in this quiet town?"

Working on automatic, she poured her tea, put a little butter in the pan, and scrambled her two eggs with a fork as they cooked. The toast popped out, one side darker than the other. The toaster had done that ever since Fiona extracted a jammed half muffin from it with a fork. But Jean didn't even consciously notice, although she put her butter and marmalade as always on the light side of the toast.

Dr. Shah ... And just when she thought she was starting to see a glimmer of light in the Kelso case. What possible relationship could there be between the deaths of Kelso and Shah, because of course there had to be one? In her mind, she saw Hugh Kirkwall's tormented face, with new, deep lines etched into it in the course of the nightmarish last week. She knew of his hatred of Shah, and also knew that it was not in his nature to hate, which made it a much more dangerous passion. People who hate a lot, and Jean knew of several, know from long habit how to deal with it, but in Hugh it was an unaccustomed emotion. Could it have led him to carry out such a monstrous act of revenge? Jean was still wondering when the phone rang. It was Douglas.

"I suppose you heard the news?" he asked.

"Just this minute. What happened?"

Douglas told her about how he and Jamieson had found Shah's body, and when he told her about the way Shah had been killed, a momentary and unexpected recollection of certain photographs she'd seen recently flashed into her head, and she gasped.

"Are you all right?" asked Douglas.

"Yes. I just thought of something . . . Have you spoken to Hugh Kirkwall?"

"Indeed we did," replied Douglas grimly. "Last night. And I'm no' sure that he'll be able to get himself out of this particular situation."

"Oh, dear. Aside from the circumstances, was there anything that led you to him?"

"The circumstances are pretty powerful, as you know. And we know for a fact that he was actually in the room where the murder took place, within minutes of Shah's death."

"How do you know that, Douglas?"

"As it happens, he told us," said Doug, rather

shortly. Jean had a way of gently deflating him that irritated Douglas, but somehow he couldn't resent it.

"Did anyone else see him there?"

"I don't know yet. I still have people to interview. Why do you ask?"

"It just occurred to me that he might be trying to protect someone, but of course that's pure conjecture on my part."

"Who?"

"I don't know. I'm just trying to think . . ."

"Are you thinking of Dr. Anna McKenzie?"

"I wasn't thinking of anyone in particular," said Jean, although for a second the image of the pretty and distraught Anna McKenzie had flashed through her mind.

"Well, I just wanted you to know what happened," said Douglas. His voice took on a resigned tone. "I have a feeling that the, uh, mud is going to hit the fan today. I have to go up to see Bob McLeod in about ten minutes . . ." Douglas sighed. "Can I come by this evening?"

"Of course. Do you want to bring Cathie over for dessert?"

"Cathie's more of a main course, actually," replied Douglas with a valiant attempt at humor. "But no, thank you kindly, Jean. She has to stay home and take care of the bairn."

"You're a chauvinist, Douglas. It would be nice for Cathie to get out of the house from time to time, don't you think?"

"I'll ask her," said Douglas, but without enthusiasm.

Jean heard his words, but when she put the phone down, the thought of Dr. Shah's almost-severed head was occupying most of her mind, whirling around in her imagination like the dark, fast-moving cloud that heralds a tornado, and threatens to obliterate everything in its path.

After breakfast, Jean called the surgery for her home visits, and after getting Steven and the girls off to work, she set out to see those patients who for one reason or another were unable to come down to the surgery. Jean's brother, a physician in the States, once asked Jean whether these visits were a cost-effective way of dealing with patients. "You spend more of your time driving around town rather than actually with your patients," he told her.

But Jean had defended the system. "When I see a patient in his own home," she told him, "I get a much better idea about who he is, how he interacts with his family, and what kind of a person I'm dealing with. I can see if there are money problems, if they're sloppy or over-meticulous. So when I see them later at the surgery complaining of a headache, I'm better equipped to tell if it's stress-related, or if they have back pain, if it's real, or if they're just trying to get time off work."

Her first visit was to a retired coal mine foreman with silicosis who lived in the Oakbank area, near the hospital. He was very breathless, and Jean decided that the time had come to put him on oxygen. She arranged with the local British Oxygen Company branch to bring the equipment to his home, and on the way back, decided to stop in at the hospital and see how Kitty Brewster was doing. Peter MacIntosh had told Jean that they'd put the huge fibroid in a jar and labeled it JC2, which, he said, had aroused the curiosity of the whole department.

Kitty was up and out of bed, walking around in the corridor, pushing her IV pole in front of her, looking for a nurse.

"My IV's stopped," she explained when Jean came up. She was looking flushed and concerned. "And there's never anybody around in this place, especially when you need them."

"Let's go back to your room, and I'll fix it," said Jean. The cheerful calm of her voice reassured Kitty, and she followed Jean back and sat on her bed. With a little manipulation Jean got the IV fluid running through the tubing again, and Kitty relaxed. Jean chatted with her for a few minutes; Kitty was anxious to get out of the hospital and return to her job in Edinburgh. "I phoned them yesterday," she told Jean, "and they want me back."

"That's great," said Jean. "But promise me you'll find a doctor in Edinburgh, so we can send him your records. If you want, we can find one for you." She looked at her watch. "Oops," she said. "I have to run. Now, don't you move that arm too much, Kitty, or the IV'll stop again. You should be getting out of here in a day or two, so phone me when you get home."

On the way out, Jean stopped at the nurses' desk. A nurse and an aide were talking excitedly in low tones, and Jean could guess what they were discussing. Jean visited another of her patients on the medical floor, and chatted with some of the staff. Everybody was nervous, and Jean could feel a palpable tension, a sense of insecurity and fear emanating from the personnel of the entire hospital. On the way out, she caught a glimpse of Sandy Michie, the administrator. Looking anxious and harassed, he was talking in low tones to Peter MacIntosh, who seemed equally concerned.

Outside the main hospital entrance, the clouds were gathering, and Jean could smell the rain coming. Kinnoull Hill, normally clearly visible from the hospital's elevated position, was shrouded in gray clouds, always a portent of bad weather on the way. Jean had lived long enough in Perth to feel the differences in weather that the varying winds foretold. Now, it was coming in hard, dry, puffy gusts, swirling around the corner of the administrative wing and kicking up the dust high enough to get into her eyes. For a moment she thought of Hugh Kirkwall, well over six feet tall. His head would be above the level of this upstirred dust, and he would never know what it was like to live this close to the ground.

For a moment she couldn't remember where she'd left her car, then she headed toward the main parking area. Her little red Renault was there, looking a little battered, and as she walked toward it, she remembered that John at the Shell garage on the Dunkeld Road had offered to buy it if she decided to get a new one.

Slowly, Jean unlocked the car door and opened it. Something had happened inside the hospital that was ringing some kind of insistent bell inside her head, but she couldn't quite fathom what it was. Something to do with Kitty Brewster . . . The car seat was cold, and Jean shivered, only in part from the chilly contact. A particularly strong gust of wind rocked the car slightly, and the first blast of rain from the north slashed across the windshield.

And then it hit her like a blow in the face. "Oh, no!" she said out loud, in an agony of disbelief. She held onto the steering wheel, not even seeing the waves of rain that were now almost blotting out the hospital buildings behind her.

Several minutes later, feeling suddenly old and shaking with more than the cold, she started the car and slowly drove down the hill, through the gates, and turned left into Rose Street. Now that she knew how Robertson Kelso had died, and was reasonably certain about who had done it, she still had a lot to do before the case could be considered solved. For one thing, she still had no idea how Dr. Shah's death was tied in, but she was pretty sure that now she would be able to find out.

Chapter 20

Chief Inspector Bob McLeod, Douglas's direct boss, was not in a good humor, as Douglas could tell from the moment he stepped into his office. McLeod was a pipe smoker, and a more or less direct correlation existed between the visibility in the office and his state of mind. Now Douglas could barely see across the small room, and the blue Balkan Sobranie smoke billowing from Bob's pipe reminded Doug of a film he'd seen of the eruption of Mount Saint Helens.

Bob's blue-eyed stare penetrated the gloom like twin, hostile searchlights, but he started quietly enough. "How's the Kelso case progressing?" he asked.

"Not much new to report, sir," said Douglas. "We've established that no known poisons were involved, and Dr. Anderson tells me that he sent away specimens of the heart muscle for specialized examination. These showed that he didn't have a heart attack. So we haven't been able to establish a cause of death, and that makes it difficult to move forward."

"I see." Another blast from Bob's furnace momentarily obscured his face. "So you've decided to ignore the coroner's findings."

"No, sir," replied Douglas, alarmed. "Not at all. It's that there was no weapon, nothing we could clearly identify as related to his death. So although we have a number of suspects . . ."

"And what about Dr. Shah? Are you as confused about the cause of *his* death?"

"No, sir." Douglas, taking a defensive stance, didn't comment further.

Bob's stare was getting grimmer. "I had the chief constable on the phone this morning," he said, "and he isn't happy. He couldn't understand why you hadn't made an arrest yet."

Douglas said nothing, but could feel Bob's fury gathering momentum. "Everybody in this dam' town knows who did it," Bob shouted suddenly. "It's so obvious that even your boy Jamieson could have figured it out."

Douglas merely straightened up a little. He was now standing at attention, forefingers on the seams of his trousers, eyes fixed straight ahead.

"Did you search Mr. Kirkwall's home?" asked Bob.

"No, sir."

Bob stood up suddenly, and the back of his chair smacked into the wall behind him. He put his pipe down on the heavy glass ashtray, and faced Douglas. He was bigger than Doug, with a round, crew-cut bullet head and aggressive eyes and jaw, and had made a reputation as a tough, capable officer. Now his present job was mostly administrative, and he didn't like it. His frustrations didn't come out often, but when they did, his subordinates all knew that a wise course of action was to walk softly and stay out of his way.

Now his voice was quiet, but just as threatening as before. "And why the hell not?"

"We went to his house and interviewed him soon after discovering Dr. Shah's body, sir," replied Douglas stiffly. "Mr. Kirkwall is a highly intelligent man, and would certainly have disposed of the murder weapon had he had one. Secondly, at the present time, I didn't think there was enough evidence to proceed further."

"I see. So now you've decided that the few tools we're left with in our fight against crime, such as obtaining a search warrant and *looking* for evidence in criminals' homes, are of no value."

"No, sir."

"Inspector Niven, you don't seem to realize what a rat's nest has been stirred up here. I've had the hospital administrator on the phone twice already this morning. The hospital's in an uproar, and the nurses and female employees are now refusing to come in at night without an escort. The press, Grampian Television, the superintendent, even the chief constable are on my back. Even my colleagues right here in the headquarters building are asking, 'What is Niven waiting for?' And I agree. It's as clear a case as any I've ever seen. Mr. Kirkwall took the opportunity to kill the man who had stolen his wife, then followed up with

Dr. Shah, who was trying to wreck his career. Jesus Christ, Niven, what the hell more do you want?"

"Are you ordering me to arrest Mr. Kirkwall, sir?"

Bob hesitated for a moment. "No. But you need to bring him in for questioning." He looked up at the clock behind Douglas. "Do it now," he said. "I'll call the *Courier* and the TV. Bring him in in about an hour, okay? At the main entrance here. That way it can be on the one o'clock news."

Bob hadn't picked up his pipe again, and the smoke in the office seemed to be clearing slightly. "There's a lot more to police work than catching criminals, my lad," he said in a calmer voice. "Remember, it's the public who pays our miserable salaries, and they need to see results. Now, get going."

Jean, still very shaken, made her way back to the surgery. It was still raining hard and steadily now, so there wasn't much point waiting for it to slow down. She got out of her car, opened the gate, and splashed through the puddles in the pathway to the door.

"We have to do something about those puddles out there," she said to Eleanor, a little out of breath. "Maybe we should get the path resurfaced or raised, or something."

"Good idea. Here, give me your shoes," said Eleanor, getting up from behind her desk. "I'll stuff them with newspaper, and that'll keep them from being ruined."

"How many patients do we have?"

"Just two so far. They're both here for prescription refills. We won't see many more this afternoon, not with this weather." Eleanor stared at Jean. "Are you all right?"

"I'm fine. Just a bit wet ... Eleanor, I'm going to be on the phone a lot this afternoon, so ask Dr. Inkster to see those two patients and also to take any calls, please."

In her stockinged feet, Jean padded over to her office, went in, and closed the door. A few moments later, a light lit on Eleanor's telephone console, indicating that Jean was on the phone. Eleanor gazed at the little light, and wondered what Dr. Montrose was up to now.

Jean's first call was to the hospital, and she asked to be put through to the administrator's office. Mr. Michie was in, but he sounded very preoccupied.

"Sandy, I know you're busy, I have one small question you might be able to answer. You know that Dr. Shah used to work part-time in a clinic in Dundee. Can you tell me the name of that clinic?"

"Just a moment."

Jean could hear him say something to his secretary, and a minute later he came back. "Yes. It says here that he worked at the Dundee Women's Clinic, on Caledonian Road, but only until about a year ago. I don't believe he had any other outside appointments since that time." He paused for a moment. "Jean, why do you want to know?"

"Oh, I'm just following up on a couple of things," she said vaguely. "Thank you so much, Sandy. I know how busy you are right now."

"It's like a zoo in this place," he replied gloomily. "And it's getting worse."

Jean had a Dundee phone book and quickly found the clinic's number. The first person she spoke to couldn't help her, but finally she reached the medical director, a pleasant woman, Dr. Moira Mills, whom, it turned out, Jean had once met at a conference. She didn't have the information Jean was looking for, but promised to get it for her. "Will tomorrow be all right?" she asked.

"It'll be perfect," replied Jean. "Thank you so much."

Her next call took a little more preparation; she had to draw on her reservoir of acquaintances, but finally she found where Frances Kirkwall's parents lived. As it turned out they now had a house in Aviemore, and after a little more delving in the phone books, Jean dialed the number and reached her father.

After introducing herself, she said, "I'm trying to reach Frances, and hoped you could help me."

After a brief silence, he said, "You'd better talk to her mother. If you'll wait a minute, please, she's outside, taking in the washing."

Mrs. Donoghue was not immediately helpful, and was evasive about her daughter's whereabouts.

But when Jean explained the situation, Mrs. Donoghue rather reluctantly told her that Frances was living in Glasgow. "Yes," she said. "Frances got away from that awful Kelso man a long time ago. He treated her like dirt," she went on. "And Frances only stayed a few weeks with him. She couldn't just go back to Perth, of course, so she got herself a job at the Western Infirmary in Glasgow, in the bacteriology department. Not as good as the one she had in Perth, but she's getting by."

When Jean asked if Frances had thought about going back to Hugh, her mother said, "I've wanted her to do that, and told her so. But she's so embarrassed . . . She couldn't stand the thought of coming back and having to face all these disapproving wives and colleagues."

They talked for a few more minutes; Mrs. Donoghue gave Jean Frances's home phone number, although she didn't think talking to her would help, and Jean wrote the number down on the pad, thinking that she'd phone her that evening.

Throughout the conversation, Jean felt a penetrating sadness that seemed to be getting worse, moment by moment. It was taking her entire body over, like the beginnings of a bad flu. This was one of the saddest and most terrible cases she'd ever been involved in, and it certainly wasn't over yet.

When she got home that evening, Steven and the girls were in the living room watching the television news. They had just seen footage in which Dr. Hugh Kirkwall was being escorted, white-faced, into the police headquarters building.

"To help with their inquiries," said Steven, repeating what the announcer had said. "Yeah, sure. Why can't the police call a spade a spade? They think he killed Kelso and Shah, and they've brought him in to try to make him confess, so why don't they say so?"

"Poor man, he seemed such a nice person," said the kindhearted Lisbie. "I'm sure he didn't kill anyone, did he, Mum?"

"I hope you're right, dear," said Jean. "Now, has anyone started dinner?"

"I'll do it," said Fiona. She was lying flat on her stomach, and got up slowly. "Does *beef bourguignon* sound okay to everybody?"

"I knew that was what you'd make," said Lisbie. "You made a big batch last week and froze half of it. You're just going to thaw it out and take credit for making a whole dinner."

"Well, it's more than you ever did," said Fiona, standing up and swirling her tartan skirt. "If we had to rely on your cooking, Lisbie Montrose, we'd all be looking like that old skinny model, what was her name?"

"Twiggy," said Steven, smiling.

"*Dad!*" said Lisbie, aggrieved. "That's not fair. Why do you *always* take her side?"

The door opened and Mrs. Findlay came in, thin as a wraith in a long white dressing gown. "You girls are making a lot of noise," she said, looking from Fiona to Lisbie. "You practically drowned out my TV upstairs."

"That was Lisbie," said Fiona, doing her best to sound solemn. "I'm sorry, Gran. I apologize for her."

Mrs. Findlay gazed pensively at Fiona for a moment, then turned to Jean. "So they finally caught your friend Mr. Kirkwall," she said. "I saw it on the TV. Did you know they're calling him the *killer doc*?"

"Would anyone besides Gran and Mum like a glass of sherry?" asked Steven, heading for the door.

"Yes, please," came a chorus from Lisbie and Fiona. They grinned and gave each other a quick high five, then Fiona went off to the kitchen to defrost her *boeuf bourguignon*.

Jean looked at her watch and slipped away upstairs to their bedroom to phone Frances Kirkwall. She sat on the bed for a few moments, thinking about her, and considering what she was going to say. Of course she had known Frances when she was with Hugh—they'd met at functions from time to time, and Jean and Steven had been to their house. Jean remembered her as a quiet, very capable young woman, in her mid-thirties, a bit obsessive perhaps, and a meticulous homemaker. And she had an outstanding reputation as a bacteriologist. A couple of years previously, there had been several cases of botulism in the area, two of them fatal, and Frances had tracked the deadly toxin to a shipment of Peruvian sardines. She'd started a meals-on-wheels program in Perth for people who were too old or too ill to prepare their own food, and all in all, Frances had been liked and respected in the community, until she'd been struck down by some kind of temporary insanity and gone off with Robertson Kelso.

Holding the phone, Jean shook her head. What was it about Robertson Kelso that had made women fall for him so hard? Frances must have known what an evil person he was—everybody in Perth did. But he knew how to pick his women, and for a while he could be the most charming, sympathetic, and reassuring man one could imagine. Anyway, Frances had seen through him quicker than most, and was lucky to have got out of his clutches in one piece.

Frances was home. When Jean told her who she was, Frances started to cry. Then they talked for a little while. Jean told her about the trouble that Hugh was in, and that upset her terribly. It took some persuading to get Frances to agree to Jean's plan, but finally she said she would go along with it, and she sounded a lot more cheerful by the time the two of them hung up.

At dinner, the conversation was about Hugh Kirkwall.

"I can't believe it," said Lisbie. "Did you see how sad he looked when they were taking him in? With a policeman on either side, holding his arms?"

"Of course he was sad," said Fiona mockingly. "Wouldn't you be sad if you got caught?"

"Depends on what I was caught doing." Lisbie tilted her chin up. She had an unerring way of opening herself up for trouble; Jean thought that Lisbie knew it, and did it out of some self-destructive instinct.

Fiona instantly took advantage, and fell on her sister like a shark upon mullet. "Well, for instance, how about chugalugging from the sherry bottle?" she asked.

Lisbie's eyes filled with instant tears, and she slammed her water glass on the table. "Okay," she said, "if that's how you want it, how about what you were doing downstairs on the couch with Bobby Angus last week? If you hadn't heard me coming down the stairs . . ."

"Like an elephant. There was no missing that. You make the cups rattle on the shelf and the lights swing on the ceiling."

Lisbie turned to her mother. "*Mum*, did you hear what she said?"

"Yes, dear. Now, if you'd just pass me your father's plate, please . . . Fiona, dinner was delicious, wasn't it, Steven?"

"Yes. Best beef stew I've had for ages. Was it out of a tin?" asked Steven innocently.

"I don't think he did it," said Mrs. Findlay suddenly.

"Who did what?" Jean leaned over and unobtrusively picked up a piece of beef that had fallen beside her mother's plate.

"Hugh Kirkwall. You remember Anna Talbot? The teacher at the academy? Well, he took out her gall bladder four years ago, and she did wonderfully. He wouldn't kill anybody."

"Then, who did it, Gran?" Fiona's slightly derisive tone drew a warning glance from Steven.

"It was his wife. Frances."

Jean stared at her. "How do you know that, Mother?" she asked quietly.

"It's obvious. Kelso had been bad to her, as he'd been to everyone else he'd touched. And that disgusting Dr. Shah was trying to ruin Hugh. So she killed him so that Hugh would take her back."

There was a stunned silence, broken quickly by Steven, mostly so that neither of the girls would have a chance to offend Mrs. Findlay. "I imagine Inspector Niven must have considered that possibility," he said gravely, but when he glanced at Jean, to his astonishment she seemed to have gone a bit pale. "Are you all right, dear?" he asked her, concerned.

"Yes, of course." Anxious to change the subject, she turned to Lisbie. "How is May doing?" she asked. "You haven't said anything about her for a few days."

"She's all right," replied Lisbie. "She had an attack yesterday, though, and she took a long time to get over it."

"Would you like to invite her for dinner again?" An idea struck Jean. "How about tomorrow?"

"I'll ask her mother," said Lisbie, smiling happily. "Thanks, Mum."

At that moment they all heard the sound of the doorbell.

"It's him! The love of my life!" cried Fiona. She got up so quickly her chair would have fallen if Steven hadn't caught it. She ran to open the door, and sure enough, Douglas's amused voice was heard in the hall, then he appeared in the doorway, with Fiona hanging onto his arm.

"I'm not staying," he said, absently patting Fiona's forearm. "Jean, I just wanted you to know that we just now arrested Mr. Kirkwall for the murders of Robertson Kelso and Dr. Ramashandra Shah."

That night, Jean went to bed late, later than she needed to. She wandered around the quiet house after everyone else had retired, clipping the faded geranium blossoms on the kitchen windowsill, washing a few items of cutlery that had escaped the dishwasher, and doing little household jobs here and there that didn't really need to be done. Finally she went softly upstairs, walking to the side of the second-from-the-top step that creaked so loudly.

She climbed into her side of the bed, and Steven stirred, mumbled something, turned, and went back to sleep.

Jean lay on her back, watching the shadows moving to and fro on the ceiling. A tree stood between the streetlight and the bedroom, and the light breeze outside made the pattern of leaves move in a slow, soporific way, crisscrossing to and fro, and Jean thought about Douglas, about Kelso and Shah, and about what her mother had so astonishingly said. Then she tried to put in perspective the sudden flash of understanding that she'd had outside the hospital. How had she not thought of it sooner? All the indications had been there, and the fact that neither Douglas nor Malcolm Anderson had tumbled to it didn't excuse her.

A sad vision of Hugh Kirkwall came to her, tormented, distraught, caught in and reacting to a turmoil not of his own making, and now in prison. A profound feeling of pity came over her. And she had promised him to do what she could ... She thought about trying to visit him in the morning, but decided not to. For one thing she had a lot to do the next day, and, knowing Hugh, he would be so embarrassed to be seen in prison clothes and in custody that a visit from her would simply add to his ordeal.

Chapter 21

The next day dawned gray and threatening. Jean woke to the sound of wind and rain beating against the windowpanes of the bedroom, like witches tapping and howling to get in. She had been dreaming about floods, torrents racing down huge open ditches, carrying trees and chicken coops and livestock in their path. But the torrents were of blood ... She climbed out of bed, shivering with the fast-disappearing recollection. Glancing back at Steven to make sure she hadn't wakened him, Jean pulled on her old terry cloth dressing gown and went into the bathroom. When she emerged she was ready for the day, looking good in an almost-new gray cashmere-and-wool dress with a simple white collar, and a slim black belt with round silver ornaments. Black hose and shoes completed the outfit. Jean turned sideways to check her profile. She pulled in her tummy, sighed, and went downstairs to wake the girls.

Her mother was already in the kitchen. She had made her usual tea and dry toast for herself, not a breakfast that Jean would have particularly enjoyed. Mrs. Findlay silently watched her daughter take butter and jam, then two eggs and bacon out of the refrigerator.

"Jean, have you ever noticed that there are no fat old people?" she asked.

"No I haven't," said Jean, her mind on other things. She looked through the window; the rain was still coming down, and Mr. Forrest's prize sheep were standing in the middle of the field next to the house, huddled together in a stoic, wet, and despondent-looking little flock.

"Well, it's true. Thin people live longer, healthier, and happier lives." Mrs. Findlay took a noisy sip of tea. "Dear me, Jean, you're a doctor, you should know that."

Jean thought about the many old people she knew, and had to admit there was some truth in what her mother was saying. "At that rate, Mother, you should live forever," she said.

"It wasn't me I was thinking about," snapped Mrs. Findlay. "And anyway, I don't want to live for ever. I don't have anything to live for anymore, so I'm ready to go anytime. Today, if the Lord wishes it."

"Please, Mother, not today," said Jean, smiling. "I already have a really difficult day ahead."

"I doubt whether He'll take your schedule into consideration when the Time Comes," said Mrs. Findlay acidly. She poured herself another cup of tea. "So what are you going to do today that's so important? Swoop in on a helicopter and snatch Mr. Kirkwall from the clutches of the law?"

"Hardly." Jean was already tensing up at the thought of the things she did have to do, although they weren't quite as daring as what her mother had suggested. Dr. Moira Mills, at the Dundee Women's Clinic, had said she'd call her at nine-thirty with the information she needed, and come hell or high water Jean was going to be in her office at nine-twenty-five, waiting.

Fiona appeared at the door, holding her dressing gown tightly around her, looking a bit like an otter who'd been in the water too long, with her black hair sticking out all over her head, and her unmade-up face pale and shiny.

"Well, you are a pretty sight this morning, miss," said Mrs. Findlay, looking her granddaughter over. "The cat's left better-looking things on our doorstep many a time."

"Lisbie's been in the bathroom forever," complained Fiona. "I think she must have got her bottom stuck in the seat."

"There's no need to be crude, dear," said Jean. "You can use the upstairs bathroom if you want."

"Thanks, but all my stuff's downstairs," said Fiona, gritting her teeth. "One day I'm going to kill that girl."

"Or, of course, you could just set your alarm and get up a few minutes before Lisbie," suggested Jean. "I'm sure she'll be out soon. Here, have a cup of tea while you're waiting."

The crisis was solved when Lisbie appeared in the doorway a few moments later, looking her usual fresh, cheerful, and smiling self. Fiona growled something at her that was fortunately un-intelligible to Jean and Mrs. Findlay, and disap-peared down the stairs.

By eight, everyone was ready to leave the house, and Mrs. Findlay had gone back upstairs to her room with the newspaper, already folded open at the obituary columns.

Jean had a couple of home visits to do before going to the surgery. She picked up her big black bag and hefted it into the car. Until a few months before, she used to leave her medical bag in the car, but her partner Helen Inkster had recently had her car broken into and the thieves had gone off with her bag, so nowadays Jean always brought hers in at night.

The first visit was to an old man who was in agony because he couldn't urinate, but he was too embarrassed to allow Jean to examine him, so she phoned for an ambulance and sent him in to the hospital. Her second visit was to see Betsy Clarke, a little asthmatic girl who had inadvertently helped Jean track down the killer of Hector Mur-doch, who had lived across the street. The FOR SALE sign was still up outside Hector's old home. No wonder, thought Jean. Nobody who knew the story would ever want to live there.

Betsy's mother had called just as Jean was leav-ing home, and she sounded distressed. "She's re-ally bad this time," she told Jean. "Last time she got like this Dr. Inkster had to put her in the hos-pital and they started her on steroids."

Jean rang the doorbell; from where she stood

on the doorstep, she could hear Betsy wheezing inside. She sounded terrible, and Jean mentally calculated the dose of Prednisone a ten-year-old would require. Jean didn't like giving such powerful medications to a child, but sometimes there was no other way of breaking an asthma attack. Betsy's mother, a thin, harassed-looking young woman in a print apron, opened the door and let Jean into the flat. Betsy was in the little bedroom she shared with her brother, who was at school. A thin child, Betsy was sitting up in bed, panicked, wide-eyed, breathing with a lot of difficulty, her nostrils dilating with every breath, clutching at the bedclothes with her thin little hands.

Jean sat down on the bed, took Betsy's hand, and talked quietly to her for a few moments. Sometimes Betsy would get herself so worked up that her asthma just got worse and worse. Then Jean listened to her chest. The wheezes and rattles in her lungs were audible even without the stethoscope. Betsy was having a really bad attack, and having great difficulty getting air in and out of her lungs. Putting her stethoscope away, and pulling a small bottle of Prednisone pills out of her bag to count out a starter dose for the child, Jean asked if Betsy had been using her inhaler normally. Betsy nodded. She was an intelligent child, and certainly knew how to use the inhaler. On a hunch, Jean reached over and picked up the small blue Ventolin inhaler from the bedside table. It felt lighter than usual, and Jean shook it, then depressed the cylinder.

"Have you been using this much?" she asked Betsy.

"Yes, but it's not helping anymore," whispered Betsy. "Not since last night."

"It's empty," said Jean, smiling. "That's why. Let me see, now ... I think I probably have one in my bag."

She did. Five minutes later, Betsy's breathing was almost back to normal, and she was wanting to get out of bed.

Well, that saved the National Health Service some money, thought Jean as she drove back to her surgery. She could feel her heart starting to pound, thinking about Dr. Mills's call. Would she remember to phone? Supposing her hunch was totally wrong? It wouldn't be the first time, but it would totally invalidate the entire premise she'd built up. She looked at her watch. Nine-fifteen. She couldn't have timed it better.

Jean was telling Eleanor that when the call came through she wasn't to be disturbed under any circumstance, when Helen, her partner, came out of her office. "There's a child I'd like you to see. . . ." she started, but Jean interrupted as politely as she could. "I'm sorry, Helen, but it'll have to wait. I have a call coming in now that I have to take. . . ."

The phone rang. "It's a Dr. Mills for you," said Eleanor. Jean almost ran into her office and closed the door, her heart beating wildly.

"Well, I think I have the answers to all your questions, Jean," said Dr. Mills. She had a pleasant, matter-of-fact voice, and Jean felt that this was a woman she'd like to get to know better.

Jean sat down and picked up a pencil. Her hand was shaking. Five minutes later, Jean replaced the phone in its cradle, sat back, and took what felt like her first breath since she picked the phone up. Then the wave of expected sadness came over her. The worst part of this case was still to come, she knew it.

Chapter 22

The papers were full of Hugh Kirkwall's arrest, and the case of the killer doc had made it into the national press. The *Mirror*'s headline was simply GOTCHA, DOC! while those of other more sedate publications ranged from DOCTOR DEATH TRAPPED to MAD SURGEON STRIKES AGAIN, NAILED.

Jean was kept busy most of the day. She made several phone calls, gleaning little bits of information here and there, all building on to the facts she had already confirmed. Finally, she put in a call to Douglas Niven. He didn't return her call until late in the afternoon. He was apologetic, but even then, the self-satisfaction in his voice was unmistakable. He'd been tied up with the Kirkwall business all day, and Bob McLeod had needed a long briefing to prepare for a press conference scheduled for early the next morning.

Jean took a deep breath, and told Doug what she had to say. When she finished, there was a long silence. So long that Jean finally said, "Douglas, are you all right?"

Doug's voice was barely recognizable. "Yes, of

course I'm all right. It's just . . . Jean, how in the name of God did you figure all that out?" he asked, almost in a whisper. But he seemed to gain strength as he talked. "And anyway, it's really just conjecture. What you said is very interesting, but it doesn't sound as if you have any proof, not proof that would stand up in court, anyway."

"Douglas, I'm not in the slightest bit interested in whether proof stands up in court or on its hind legs or anywhere else. All I'm interested in are the facts, and those I'm pretty sure of. Now, this is what I think we should do . . ."

When Jean finished, Douglas said, "Jean, I'm sorry, but the answer is no. Absolutely No. For one thing, you'd be exposing yourself to personal danger, and secondly this is a matter for the police to follow up, and not for private individuals like yourself."

"I did consider that, Douglas," said Jean quietly, "but don't you see, this is probably the *only* way that we can actually prove it. As you said, it's mainly conjecture, together with a good dollop of circumstantial evidence. I hope you'll be able to find some more durable proof, and I have some ideas about that, too. Meanwhile, I think we should go ahead along the lines I mentioned."

After a few more minutes of discussion, Douglas reluctantly agreed to Jean's suggestion. They decided when and where they would meet, and Douglas promised to bring the necessary equipment.

Jean felt hugely relieved that she'd passed at

least some of the responsibility to Douglas, and when she got into her car to go home, she tried to put the matter out of her mind. Her petrol gauge was low, so she stopped at the Shell garage on the Dunkeld Road, where she usually went. John was there, big and cheerful as ever. Although it was self-service, he came out when he saw her car and pumped the petrol for her.

"I see you still haven't sold your Renault," he said. "My offer's still open."

"Thanks, John," she said, smiling. "As soon as I can afford a new one, you'll be the first to know."

Jean drove down Atholl Street, turned left, and was lucky enough to find a parking space beyond the old town library, near the back entrance to Marks and Spencers. She ran in, bought a fillet of fresh salmon, some small new potatoes, a lemon, a big bunch of parsley, asparagus, a box of green foil-covered mints, strawberries, and a pint of double cream for dessert.

"Where on earth do you manage to get straw- berries from at this time of year?" she asked the attractive young woman at the checkout counter. The girl stared at Jean as if she'd asked her to explain the theory of relativity.

"No idea," she said. "That'll be twenty-three pounds and twelve p."

As Jean had expected, only Mrs. Findlay was home when she came in with her parcels, and she was upstairs in her room watching television.

For the next while, Jean busied herself in the kitchen. She turned on the oven and preheated it, then wrapped the salmon in foil, after sprinkling it with parsley and pouring a couple of table-spoons each of sherry and lemon juice over it.

After that there were quite a few interruptions, and some quiet comings and goings. Jean broke off the lower stems of the asparagus and put them in the steamer. Fiona came home, almost on the heels of her father. Jean talked with them for a few minutes, then went back to her cooking. Lisbie came in with May, stayed in the kitchen for a few moments, then they went off downstairs to listen to some new CDs that Lisbie had bought.

Fiona reappeared in the kitchen. "Shall I make the potatoes?" she asked.

"That would be nice of you, dear," said Jean. "I was going to make Barbies."

"That's my favorite," said Fiona. "That way you don't have to peel them."

Jean's mother had taught her to make Barbie potatoes as a young girl. Nobody knew where the name had come from; somebody had once suggested that Ken had liked them that way. Fiona opened the bag of little red potatoes, cut them in quarters, and put them in a pan, already half full of boiling water. Twenty minutes later, she emptied the water out, added a chunk of butter and some parsley flakes to the potatoes, and stirred the whole thing up with a fork. "Ready," she said.

"Good. The salmon's ready, and so is the asparagus. Would you like to call everybody?"

A few minutes later they were all sitting around the table, talking and laughing. Steven recounted a meeting with a group of Japanese businessmen who had visited his glassworks that day. They had been very polite, with lots of bowing and smiling, but Steven hadn't understood a single word they said. Then they took photographs and went away, still smiling and bowing. Steven didn't know if they'd bought the entire works, placed a huge order, or gone off with his trade secrets.

Jean kept an eye on May. She was a beautiful girl, but had the mind of a four-year-old, with an attention span of only a few moments. She couldn't feed herself without making a mess around her, and had to be helped to drink from a glass. But she seemed happy enough—she loved Lisbie, and a couple of times during dinner kissed her loudly on the cheek, to Fiona's quiet hilarity.

Dessert was a success, too.

"Where do you think they get strawberries at this time of year?" asked Steven, echoing Jean's question to the sales assistant. Jean told them about the salesgirl's response, and everybody laughed, except Mrs. Findlay.

"You couldn't have answered any more intelligently than she did, Jean," she said. "So that wasn't very funny."

After dinner, everybody went their own way, and Jean went into the living room to do some paperwork.

Half an hour later, Fiona had just come in to ask if she'd like some tea, when the doorbell rang and Jean went to answer it. It was Rosemary Gallacher, looking her usual calm and capable self, coming to pick up her daughter.

"Come in, come in," said Jean. "Let me take your coat. Fiona was just going to make some tea."

Rosemary gave Jean a friendly peck on the cheek and came into the living room.

"I saw John this afternoon," said Jean, indicating the green winged chair for Rosemary to sit in. "He still wants to buy my wee car."

Rosemary sat down and put her big leather purse at her feet.

"I wish he'd just put a new set of tires on mine," said Rosemary, shaking her head. "But it's the cobbler's son who goes without shoes, isn't it?"

"Or his wife," smiled Jean.

Fiona came in with a tray, and then left, saying she had work to do.

Jean poured. "There's a lot of excitement these days up at the hospital, isn't there?" she asked. "Sugar and milk?"

"Yes, please, one lump. Yes. Everybody feels very sorry for poor Mr. Kirkwall. I suppose he was just pushed beyond his limit of tolerance, first by Kelso and then by Dr. Shah."

"Yes, I'm sure that's true . . ." Jean took a deep breath, feeling her heart beating at least twice its usual speed. "But of course he didn't kill either of them."

"Well, of course we all hope that he's found not

guilty," said Rosemary in the level tone that had reassured so many scared patients.

"You know, Rosemary, it took me ages to figure out how Robertson Kelso had been killed," said Jean. "I've never felt so stupid." She crossed her ankles and folded her hands in her lap to keep them from shaking.

"Nobody else seems to know, either, so you're in good company." Rosemary smiled, and took a sip of tea. Her hand didn't shake, not one little bit. She was steady as a rock, and for a moment Jean felt a sudden apprehension. Had her instincts and intellect let her down? This woman wasn't acting like a guilty person, not in the slightest degree.

"Oh, but I know now," said Jean. She licked her dry lips.

For the first time, Rosemary seemed to turn her full attention to Jean. "So how was it done?" she asked.

"Well, as you know, when Robertson Kelso came out of the operating room, he had two big intravenous cannulas, one in each arm. They were wide gauge, because Anna McKenzie had had to run in a lot of fluid quickly during the operation. Now, if the fluid could run *in* quickly, it could run *out* just as fast."

Rosemary stared at Jean, and sat back in her chair. "How?" she asked.

"By taking the two IV bottles off the poles and putting them under the bed," replied Jean. "That way the blood would drain out of his veins into the bottle by gravity. They were liter bottles, and he bled to death, probably quite quickly, certainly within an hour, into those bottles. That's why they didn't find any blood in him at the autopsy."

Rosemary's eyes widened. "Good heavens," she said. "I would never have thought of that."

"The bottles would have been emptied into the sink," went on Jean. "And replaced with fresh bottles of saline, and that would have taken only a minute or two, if the person was familiar with the equipment."

"If that's true, any one of half-a-dozen people could have done it." Now Rosemary's voice had a strange quality to it, and she was watching Jean with an amused expression that somehow didn't seem quite genuine.

"Right. Actually four. Dr. Shah, Anna McKenzie, Hugh Kirkwall, and you."

"Me?" Rosemary paused, and smiled. "And what about Kelso's wife? And Albert Caie?"

"Neither of them would know enough to do something like that. And people were coming in from time to time to check Kelso until after Mrs. Kelso had gone home."

"It looks as if the police decided that it was Mr. Kirkwall."

"It's a funny thing," said Jean reflectively. "Sometimes you hear something, but it doesn't click in place until something else happens ... Well, of course, what was puzzling me to begin with was *how* Kelso died, and as you said, there were lots of people who could have done it. People with strong motives, too."

Jean passed the plate of biscuits to Rosemary, who took a piece of shortbread. "Fiona made that," said Jean. "She's really a very good cook." She took a deep breath. "Anyway, something happened that I missed completely at the time, although I was told about it. When Kelso's operation was finished, Hugh Kirkwall wanted to put him in Intensive Care, but you said there weren't any beds, so he had to go to an ordinary private room. But, Rosemary, at that time there were *two* empty beds in the ICU. It *had* been full, but two patients had been transferred late that afternoon. And as supervisor, you would have known about it."

"I really don't remember," said Rosemary. Her eyes had taken on a strange glitter, and, watching her, Jean felt her mouth go dry again.

"Of course, Kelso couldn't have died that way in the ICU because there were nurses there all the time, and they'd have noticed the IV bottles under the bed, so he had to be in a private room," went on Jean. "But even if someone had figured out how it was done, it wasn't until Dr. Shah was killed that it became clear who had been responsible."

"You're saying it was the same person? My goodness, once again you're agreeing with the police."

Jean ignored the faintly sarcastic overtones in Rosemary's voice.

"Sort of. Which brings us, very sadly, to your

daughter May. She's just a delightful young woman, you know. So affectionate—and Lisbie loves her."

A change was taking place in Rosemary's face; her expression had turned dark, guarded, and her eyes didn't leave Jean's. "So what about May?"

"You and John must have been so proud of her," said Jean, chugging along her own track like a little train. "Good at school, prizes every year. And so pretty . . ." Without giving Rosemary time to respond, she went on, "And then she took that summer job at Robertson Kelso's salmon hatchery. No wonder he was attracted to her, a beautiful fifteen-year-old, and I suppose that to May he was a powerful and attractive man. I don't know how he did it, or how long it took to seduce her, but he got her pregnant . . ." Jean shook her head. "That must have been a terrible time for all of you. But you knew about that clinic in Dundee, although you probably didn't know that Dr. Shah worked there on a part-time basis."

Rosemary said nothing, but kept on staring at Jean, who felt there was something really frightening about Rosemary, who was just sitting there, unnaturally still, gazing at her with that stony square face.

"And Dr. Shah did her abortion, but he botched it. Well, maybe I shouldn't say that, because accidents can happen to anyone, but one way or another, she got a blood clot, which traveled up into her brain, with the sad results that will last all through her life."

Rosemary spoke for what seemed the first time. "A lot of what you've been saying is nonsense, of course, but Dr. Shah *did* botch it. They had an inquiry, and they threw him out of the clinic."

"Yes. Of course that's part of the public record ... Anyway, when you killed Dr. Shah with the wire, you had completed your revenge for what the two of them had done to May." Jean unclasped her hands. She'd been holding them so tightly that the fingers of both hands were numb. "You know, Rosemary," she went on, "I've been thinking a lot about this. If the same thing had happened to one of my girls, I don't know what I would have done, but I'd have made sure something drastic happened to them."

Rosemary stood up. A big woman, she towered over Jean. "You have a great imagination, Jean," she said. "And you're very clever. But the case against Mr. Kirkwall is at least as strong, and he's the one who's in jail right now. So now, if you don't mind, I'll get May and we'll be on our way home."

Jean stood up, her knees shaking so much that she almost fell. Desperately, she decided to play her last card. It wasn't even an ace, but it was all she had.

"Mr. Kirkwall will be out of jail tomorrow," she said. "You see, they found the wire that killed Dr. Shah."

"No they didn't," said Rosemary quickly, and her eyes dropped to the leather bag still at her feet.

Jean leaned down quickly and pressed the little button that Douglas had attached earlier to the side of her chair, and within a few seconds Doug opened the door and came in, followed by Jamieson and a young female police officer.

Rosemary fought. She was strong, and determined that nobody was going to touch her bag. A lamp fell over, the coffee table overturned, upsetting all the tea things. Jamieson got a punch in the neck that made him groggy, while Jean, terrified, stood in the far corner of the room, her hand over her mouth, unable to say anything, even to scream.

Finally, Rosemary was subdued. The woman officer got her hands behind her back and put handcuffs on them, and while Jamieson stood and rubbed his neck, Douglas picked up the leather bag. Rosemary loosed a kick that could have broken his arm, but the female officer twisted her arms until she stayed still.

The wire was coiled in a side pocket, attached to two hardwood handles.

Chapter 23

It turned out that the garrote had been made in John Gallacher's garage. The cut ends of the wire matched those of one of several rolls of wire hanging from pegs in the shop. Although at first the wire looked clean, the lab found minute traces of blood, which exactly matched that of Dr. Shah. John, the former SAS sergeant, had trained Rosemary in the use of the device. It was a quick, tidy technique, not messy, and all over in a minute.

"Why on earth was she still carrying that wire around with her?" Jean asked Douglas two days later.

"It's amazing, I know," replied Doug. "But killers tend to hang on to the weapons they've used, even though doing that can bring them to boot. It happens again and again."

"Like the serial killers who like to keep souvenirs of the people they killed? Pubic hair, driving licences, that kind of thing?"

"I suppose so ... Jean, it was nice of you to take May in."

"Rosemary's sister is coming up from Portsmouth to pick her up later today," replied Jean. "We'll all miss her, especially Lisbie."

"You know we let Mr. Kirkwall go, don't you?"

"Yes." Jean looked at her watch. "Actually, I'm on my way to have lunch with him."

Five minutes later, after a brisk walk along to South Street, Jean climbed up the two short flights of stairs to the Theatre restaurant. It was crowded, but she saw that Hugh was there already, sitting facing her at a table in the far corner. He saw her and raised his hand, and Jean slipped out of her coat and made her way between the tables to where he was. Hugh stood up, courteous as ever, and Jean gave him a big, heartfelt hug before sitting down in the chair he'd been sitting in. He looked faintly astonished, but Jean smiled and said, "I like to watch the people—I hope you don't mind."

"Not one little bit."

They talked for a little while, comfortably, like the old friends they were. Jean kept looking over his shoulder, but he was looking at the menu and didn't notice.

Jean saw the woman come in, and her heart quickened. She recognized the red curls, and the nice figure in the tight-fitting black coat. The woman looked very hesitant, but when she saw Jean, she smiled nervously and started to come over toward them. When she had almost come up behind Hugh, Jean smiled and said, "Hugh, there's someone behind you who's very anxious to see you."

Hugh turned his head, saw her, then jumped up in a single bound. "Oh, my God," he said, his voice shaking. "Frances!"

Jean stood up. "I just realized I have another appointment," she said, taking her coat off the back of her chair. Hugh had his arm around Frances's waist, and she was smiling as if it were the happiest moment of her life.

"*Bon appetit!*" said Jean, then she headed for the door, a little, round, unobtrusive figure, struggling into her old brown woolen coat as she made her way between the tables.

Enter C. F. Roe's world
of mystery and murder by
reading the other suspenseful
Dr. Montrose novels found on
the following pages. . . .

A Torrid Piece of Murder

A hotbed of suspicion ...

Even before the young choir singer was found dead, rumors about illicit relationships had disrupted the peace at the beautiful Scottish church attended by Dr. Jean Montrose. The body, still warm, was discovered in a sleeping bag near the front pew, and his death looked like a plausible suicide. But Dr. Montrose's instincts told her it was murder—especially since the pathologist failed to find an obvious cause of death. Now it was up to Perth's Detective Inspector Douglas Niven to do most of the investigating of a bachelor minister and his suspected appetites; the victim's pretty mother and her lover; his doctor father, who was under threat of a malpractice suit; the love-struck church secretary; and the secretive, foul-tempered organist. And soon Niven had a hunch who did it, but it was Dr. Montrose who uncovered the horrifying truth behind this mysterious death. It took her medical expertise and understanding of human nature to unravel the web of deadly deceit that drove someone to cold-blooded murder.

A Fiery Hint of Murder

The gentleman is for burning. . . .

The strange heat wave that hit Scotland had people whispering about witches, spells, and the supernatural . . . and so did the death of Morgan Stroud, science master at St. Jude's School for Boys. Dr. Jean Montrose had examined many corpses, but Stroud's mortal remains gave her chills. His body was burned to ashes, yet his hands and feet were untouched by the flames. The coroner proclaimed it a rare case of spontaneous human combustion. Detective Inspector Douglas Niven of the Perth police quietly disagreed. He knew Morgan Stroud had given many people—from his ex-wife to a former prizefighter to a boy dabbling in black magic—reasons to want him dead. But only Dr. Montrose suspected how this near-perfect crime was committed . . . and why the most volatile fuel for murder was a wounded heart.

A Bonny Case of Murder

To catch a killer ...

Caroline Fraser is undeniably a beauty and knows exactly how to use her looks to get what she wants, especially when it comes to men. But this time her self-confidence forces the hand of the wrong person, and she winds up viciously murdered with a common kitchen knife. This baffling case compels Inspector Doug Niven to turn to Dr. Jean Montrose, who was Caroline's doctor and liked her very much.

Caroline aroused strong feelings in everyone who knew her, and this only makes Niven's job tougher. His growing list of suspects includes her ex-boyfriend, Brian, who couldn't accept that he'd been given the heave-ho ... her brother, Marco, whose feelings for her were disturbingly unfamilial ... her boss, Mac, whose interest in her was unprofessional ... and the terribly jealous other secretary, Aileen. To catch the killer, Niven must investigate this uneasy set of relationships. But when his prime suspect is gruesomely murdered, he once again calls on Dr. Jean Montrose, whose expert medical knowledge and understanding of human nature are desperately needed to unravel the web of deceit and death.

A Nasty Bit of Murder

Only the victim was not under suspicion. . . .

Dr. Jean Montrose had made her house calls to Lord Aviemore's estate many times. Only this time the visit was dreadfully different. Inside the elegant mansion the damaged and lifeless body of the blue-blooded heir was a terrible sight. Detective Inspector Doug Niven of the Perth police suspected the victim's father, Dempster Lumsden, ex-playboy, confirmed alcoholic, and unfaithful husband to his beautiful society wife.

But with Dempster mysteriously missing, Dr. Jean Montrose—a tiny dynamo of a physician, who combined an expertise in forensics with a skill in snooping—turned her experienced eyes toward the Lumsdens' glittering circle of young aristocrats. What she found beneath the golden facade of the Scottish gentry were tarnished souls and shocking sins . . . but what she searched for was the one heart dark enough to kill.

A Classy Touch of Murder

Murder of a ladies' man . . .

A red Porsche was an appropriately classy vehicle for a smashup at a Scottish castle. The surprise was that the driver, Graeme Ferguson, had died from a .38 bullet neatly placed in his head. Engaged to the Earl of Strathalmond's eldest daughter, Graeme had more than his share of enemies— thanks to his lifestyle of recreational drugs, shady financial deals, and pretty women.

Now, with the investigation beginning at Strathalmond Castle itself, Detective Inspector Douglas Niven of the Perth police—working class and proud of it—felt both antagonistic and uncomfortable in the baronial halls. So he was delighted when Dr. Jean Montrose agreed to come along and offer her sharp insights into the psychology of murder. Neither sleuth expected the twists this case would take. For just like the grand estate's baffling boxwood maze, the deviousness behind this murder would lead them to one dead end and one dead body after another before its chilling solution.

A Relative Act of Murder

The lady's last lover . . .

A dead body is horrifyingly altered after a week in Scotland's River Tay. Nevertheless, Dr. Jean Montrose is fetched to the crime scene at dawn. She barely recognizes her patient, once-beautiful Moira Dalgleish, young widow, mother of a six-month-old son, and daughter of Perth's finest family.

Everyone assumes one of Moira's many lovers has done her in. But Detective Inspector Douglas Niven, smarting over orders to tread lightly in this sensitive case, wants Dr. Montrose's opinion of Moira's life among her blue-blooded kin. Soon Dr. Montrose is rubbing shoulders with the upper crust to examine dark secrets and deadly lies. She must also confirm a medical suspicion, and put into operation a risky plan that may catch a killer—or make the next corpse Niven finds her own.

A Hidden Cause of Murder

Dr. Jean Montrose deals with human weakness and death as a natural part of her profession. But the blood running from under Dr. Diane Shulman's office door suggests something very unnatural. Scotland's Dr. Montrose is terrified when she finds her partner's body. The young physician was a difficult colleague, disrupting their shared office by treating drug addicts and alcoholics. Now she fears Diane's choice of patients got her killed.

Perth Detective Inspector Douglas Niven thinks something else may have led to Diane's murder—like the malpractice that caused a distraught patient to threaten her life. Unfortunately the only person with means, motive, and opportunity is Dr. Montrose herself. In danger of being indicted, Jean Montrose realizes the case needs her expert diagnosis of the hidden causes of this brutal killing: bare bones of jealousy, dangerous secrets of the heart, and wicked passions of the flesh that usually begin with love.